THE PROUD OLD NAME

and

NOT SO, BOLIVIA

THE PROUD OLD NAME

and

NOT SO, BOLIVIA

by

Charles Elbert Scoggins

original illustrations by

W. H. D. Koerner

SPECIAL ANNOTATED EDITION

edited by

Connor MacKenzie

cover illustration by

Daniel Wood

LBME Publishing

A Note From the Editor

This book is lovingly dedicated to Joe and Nico,
who laugh at the same jokes I do.

Preface

The two books reprinted in this volume were written according to the sensibilities of the early 20th Century. Certain references to women, races, nationalities, languages, etc., may be considered inappropriate today, but were acceptable when the stories were written.

This edition presents the original text exactly as written in the 1920s so that the reader may absorb the flavor of the place and the times.

Some words reflect the spelling of a century ago and are not typographical errors, including:

- good-by
- to-day
- suit-cases
- hair-cut
- drug-store
- dining-room
- vender, an alternate spelling of 'vendor'

Scoggins also omitted accent marks in Spanish words.

Footnotes and and other supplementary material are added to enhance the reading experience, especially for those readers unfamiliar with the place and times.

ACKNOWLEDGMENTS

Ian Tregillis and his amazing slang dictionary, for his kind and gracious assistance with 1920s flapper slang.

Brenda Black Watson, Genealogist. (Lois Durham Scoggins is in her family tree.)

Rose Lynn, my intrepid writing assistant.

Phi Delta Gamma fraternity and the Phi Delta Gamma magazine archives online, from which I gathered many biographical details of Scoggins' life.

Thomas B. Costain, who introduced me to Scoggins in the first place.

The Saturday Evening Post for originally publishing The Proud Old Name, and for their delightful online archive.

And, as always, my heartfelt thanks to Lon Böder, Penney Knightly, and Liam Kincaid, for the many hours of brainstorming and all the encouragement and support, without which this volume would never have come to be.

Table of Contents

The Proud Old Name

Foreword

This is a love story.

I first discovered this amazing story in a collection of short stories and novellas that I swiped from my father's bookshelf as a teenager, way back in the 1970s, entitled *Read With Me*, edited by Thomas B. Costain. I was already a Costain fan, having shortly before discovered *The Black Rose*, perhaps one of the most romantic stories ever told.

In his introductory remarks to *The Proud Old Name*, Mr. Costain recalls working as a story scout for *The Saturday Evening Post* and relates his visit to C. E. Scoggins' literary agents, Brandt and Brandt in New York. "Scog has done it," one of the Brandt brothers (Mr. Costain wasn't sure which one) exclaimed. "He's written a novelette this time, and it's packed full of romance."

Mr. Costain read it on the train on his way back to Philadelphia, and found it to be everything Brandt had described. *The Saturday Evening Post* published it in 1923 and "it became the real beginning of" Scoggins' career. A contemporary review called it "a commendable bit of literature. Homely humor, lively narrative, abundant action, and real plot, a very large book done up in a small package."

I fell in love with the story the first time I read it. Today, over fifty years later, it's still among my most beloved tales. Set in the mining country of post-revolutionary Mexico, the history and detail are exquisite, offering a feel for the zeitgeist of the place and times in much the same way as O. Henry offers the glowing aura of the last decades of the glorious Golden Age of New York.

When *The Proud Old Name* came into the public domain, I spoke with my publisher about the possibility of releasing it under the LBME imprint. He expressed concern about the age of the story. Would modern English-speaking readers feel any connection to century-old characters in a foreign land? We batted the idea about for some months, until he finally suggested an 'enhanced' edition,' with a Scoggins biography and a brief description of the mining country around Guadalajara just after the Mexican Revolution. He also thought some footnotes on the text for clarification would amplify the experience for the contemporary reader.

Without further delay, I plunged into the task. Just who was this C. E. Scoggins? And why did he write what he wrote? Little did I realize that I was embarking on a fascinating adventure of research that would take me from the archives of the University of Colorado at Boulder through the back issues of *The Phi Gamma Delta* magazine and all the way to Sea Horse Hill in Boulder, Colorado. I'm happy to report that my investment in biographical research paid off. Imagine my surprise when someone recently referred to me as the world's foremost Scoggins scholar! (I have no idea if that is true, but throughout my research, I have not encountered another Scoggins scholar. If you're out there, I'd sure like to hear from you!)

When I began, I had no preconceived notion of the man I would find. Charles Elbert Scoggins was a true man of his time. He was born in 1888 to Methodist missionary parents in Mazatlán, Sinaloa, Mexico. Before settling down, getting married, and becoming a writer, Scoggins lived and worked in Mexico and Central America, and the southern part of the United States. Among many other jobs, he sold and installed mining machinery and helped build railroads and dams in post-revolutionary Mexico. The more I got to know him, the more I realized that

Scoggins was The Real Deal—he wrote what he lived. It's only natural that his writing tended to specialize in the lives of Americans in Latin American countries.

In the first half of the 20th century, his writing was both prolific and popular: twelve novels plus numerous short stories and magazine serials. He was a regular contributor to *The Saturday Evening Post*, *The Red Book Magazine*, *Collier's*, and many others. His works inspired two motion pictures, *Tycoon* (1947) starring John Wayne and *Untamed* (1929), featuring a young Joan Crawford.

When a story is published the first time, it's all about the story itself. But when a story is republished, it's about the effect it has had on its readers over the years. For *The Proud Old Name*, it's about the effect it has had on readers for an entire century.

Mr. Costain said it perfectly back in 1965: "… the story doesn't appear dated in any respect. The struggle between the pretty American girl and the languorous Mexican heiress could have happened yesterday." Today, fifty-seven years later, and nearly a century since *The Proud Old Name* was penned, I'm sure that you, dear Reader, will fall in love with it, too.

Connor MacKenzie, Editor
California's North Coast
Spring, 2022

He Took to Riding Out —Prospecting, I Thought; But I Might Have Known

I

YES, this is the trail to Hosto[1]. See that little flock of white specks yonder? No, not down in the basin; that's old man Moreno's hacienda[2]; farther on, up under that peak with the streak of fog across it. If I was you, though, I would wait till morning. You have to go right by Moreno's and it will be dark pretty soon; and there is no sense getting yourself shot before they can see you are a white man and a stranger. Huh? Yes, there has been a little trouble. That is where I got this. No, nothing serious; it glanced off my skull. It is what comes of getting old and careless and forgetting that a man can climb a tree.

Sure I can put you up. Pablo! Take the gentleman's horse to the corral. I will be glad to have you. I am celebrating my partner's wedding and I was right lonesome until you came along.

---

1   Hosto. Although The Proud Old Name is pure fiction, it is set in the mining country of the State of Jalisco, Mexico. The town of Hosto almost certainly refers to the little town of Hostotipaquillo, Jalisco, Mexico.

2   Hacienda. A plantation or estate, Mexican style. Before the Mexican Revolution of 1910–1920, haciendas were owned by the very wealthy and worked by peons who were, for practical purposes, bound to the land like serfs in the feudal system.

Drink hearty! What is your views on matrimony, anyway? Just a minute. That was my wife, and she understands more English than you would think. You can not get her to talk it because she is afraid you would laugh, but you never know how much she gets. I never know, and I've been married twenty years.

No, there is not much trouble around here as a rule. They do not care who is president and half the time they do not know. Of course you get robbed now and then, but if you know your business it is not much worse than taxes. You let them find a little money, not too much, and give them a drink and keep your gun in sight, and they will not go too far. It is right pitiful when you come to think of it. Once these Indians owned all the land from the Isthmus[3] clear to the Mississippi, and had caves full of gold; but now a hundred dollars looks like all the money in the world to them.

No, they are not against Americans if you treat them right. It is the Spaniards that have held their face in the dirt four hundred years.

I sure am glad to see you. I could tell you was a white man five miles off by the way you sat your horse. I was sitting here celebrating my partner's—Huh? Day before yesterday. I thought I had talked him out of it, but he is a headstrong young fellow and you can not tell him anything.

I remember how I came to take a fancy to him. I had just located this claim, I remember, and I rode up to Siete Minas[4]—that's the biggest outfit in this district, thirty miles north—with some samples to be assayed, and I stayed over that night to take a hand in a poker game. Jimmy had just come down from the States to work there, and he sure was ignorant. He was just out of mining school and that was all he knew about poker.

---

3   The Isthmus. The Isthmus of Panama.
4   Siete Minas. (Seven Mines). Possibly based on nearby Cinco Minas (Five Mines).

Yes, what those hardshells[5] ran over him was plenty. A nice young fellow too; he had a soft voice and a bashful grin like he did not want to hurt anybody's feelings, and you could not tell by looking at him that he was losing. That is the way I like to see a man. And one Swede, named Oscar something, him and another fellow took to whipsawing the kid; cross-raising him, you know, which will beat any man because it gives two chances to one.

It was none of my business, but he was a nice young fellow and I kind of hated it. Once or twice I caught me a hand and horned in between them and ran them out on a limb and sawed it off; and I joshed them about playing partners, trying to put the kid wise. Oscar, he did not like it, but he did not feel like starting anything. You know how it is in a poker game: if you start talking and get called, you have got to start shooting or eat plenty of crow[6].

It was jackpots and no limit, which is no game for young fellows because they have not got the patience. Pretty soon the kid throws in his last greenback[7] for a showdown with this Swede, and he was even too innocent to make the Swede show first.

"What you got?" says Oscar, hurrying him.

"Three queens," says Jimmy, trustful.

"'Tain't enough," says the Swede. "A flush here."

And he flashes his cards, all red, and throws them face down in the discard. But the kid did not have his eyes shut. He reaches out and turns over this flush and it is four hearts and a diamond.

"This isn't a flush," says he, puzzled.

"That ain't my hand," says the Swede, careless, and pushes the cards to me, which it was my next deal.

"It's what you threw down," says Jimmy.

"That's what you say," says the Swede. "I say it ain't."

---

5 Hardshell. A hardback; a tough person that is hard to beat or wont go down easily.

6 Eat crow. Be humiliated by admitting that you are in the wrong.

7 Greenback. American dollar bill.

And he has raked in the money, and what are you going to do about it? Shoot or shut up; you know how it is in a poker game. It was raw work. Nobody else was in the pot and it was none of our business. The Swede had all the edge; all he had to do was sit and wait for the kid to make a move. But I could see the kid had never run into anything like that before. I see him getting white over the cheek bones and gathering his feet under him, and he did not have a gun—though of course Oscar would claim he did not know.

"So that's the kind of game you play!" says the kid.

I like a man that talks quiet when he is mad.

But there was no use letting him get shot over a little pot like that. I reached over and kicked him on the shin, friendly.

"Sit down, son," I says. "Mistakes will happen. Don't never fly off in the heat of the day without a blanket."

And I pushed some money over to him and started dealing real quick, because I do not like trouble. But he just sat there kind of dazed, rubbing his shin and passing the cards along. He did not know what to make of it at all. He could see I was friendly, but I reckon he had never sat in a game where you want to watch the deal and look out for cutting into crimps[8].

Pretty soon Oscar opens a nice pot for the size of it and everybody passes around to me. I give him a little raise and he comes back at me with a big one, talking loud and bold like he was making a bluff, but I could read him like a book because he was mad. He was laying for me, account of my taking up for Jimmy, and this time he had them.

"It looks like I am hooked," I says, regretful. "If I had any sense I would lay down; but not so, Bolivia! I never did have any sense and I am too old to learn. I have got to draw my card and see what happens."

So I drew one card, and he stood pat and bet the limit. I raised, and he raised, and we went at it. He would have kept raising till the last dog was hung; but finally I called.

---

8   Cutting into crimps. A method of cheating at cards.

"What you got?" says he, like he did to Jimmy.

"That ain't the question—yet," I says. "I'm calling you."

He had them, all right. He slams down a big straight flush, jack high, and reaches for the money; but I laughed in his face.

"'Tain't enough," I says. "Not so, Bolivia! Read these and bust out crying."

And I tossed him my hand, face down, and raked in the money myself. Well, sir, it was ridiculous. He could not get it through his head.

"What's this?" says he, going glassy in the eye.

"That," I says, "is a straight flush, queen high. Or so I say. Read them real careful and tell us what you think."

It was no such thing. There was not a thing in that hand, hardly two cards of the same suit. It was his own medicine; and this time it was me that had the money and him that had to start shooting or shut up.

"And don't say that ain't my hand," I says, "because I just now handed it to you, myself. How do you like it?"

And I sat back and waited for him to make a move. The boys saw something was up; they edged away from us and waited, but a minute went by and I knew he did not have the nerve. The longer you think about it the harder it is to reach for a gun when a man is watching you.

"How about it?" I says.

He croaks, "You win," and snatches up what was left of his money and starts for the door; but I stopped him.

"Whoa!" I says. "You forgot to tell the boys what was in that hand. Do you want them to think I am a crook like you?"

He could have walked out on me; you can not shoot a man in the back; but it takes nerve to turn your back, and he did not have it.

"Straight flush, queen high," he says, husky.

"Much obliged," I says. "Good-by to you!"

And I turned the cards face up on the table. The boys all whooped and yelled, but he never cracked a smile; you take a cheap crook and he can not see a joke if it is on him. He was so rattled he bumped into the door going out, and I reckon he is going yet. He was ashamed to look that kid in the eye again.

"Here you are, kid," I says. "Here is your money back, all peaceable. You see there is no use having any trouble."

But the kid only looked more miserable and pushed it back.

"No, sir," he says, "I didn't have that much. Anyway I—I don't want it. I couldn't take it. Thanks just the same."

I thought he was mad because I was babying him before the boys. So after a while I catch him in his room; but do you think I could make him take it? Not so, Bolivia! He got plumb red in the face trying to explain without hurting my feelings, but finally it dawns on me. He didn't think I had got it honest; but wasn't it the same way the Swede got it? I ask you.

I swear to you I liked it. When you get old you do not feel so sure about what is straight and what is crooked, and it makes you feel good to see a young fellow act so—so young. I made out like I was insulted, but finally I had to laugh; and Jimmy, he can always see a joke. We got to liking each other. When Siete Minas finally shut down on account of bandits, I got him to come in here with me. I needed a man with his education and he was the kind of a damn fool that I liked.

Drink hearty! Well, I was going to ask you—how do you feel about a young fellow getting married?

II

THIS is a lonesome country for a kid. I remember when I first came down here, just about his age, I pretty near went crazy sometimes. Prospectors do get kind of cracked from being by themselves; maybe you know. The hills hanging over you at night, so many stars and all so big and still that you can not seem to stay inside yourself, and nobody to talk to but the mules. The sun coming up and something driving you on again; pulling you on, over this hill and down that *barranca*[9]; something that never lets you rest. Hunting for gold! Yes, but it is something else besides. When you do make a strike you feel lost. There is nothing to hunt for after you have found it.

Something that gets into you because you are young and husky, and keeps on driving you when you are old. Concha, she never cared. That is one thing about Indians—money and comfort is nothing much to them.

But Jimmy and me, we hit it off fine. He took to calling me Uncle Lew. He used to josh Concha—that's my wife—as solemn as

---

9   Barrancas. A barranca is a steep canyon or ravine.

an owl. He called her Doña Escopeta[10] from the way she blew up like a shotgun when she was mad. She seldom knew what he was talking about, because the things that strike a white man funny are not always funny to them, but she thought he was a great boy to be paying that much attention to her. He had a good head for mining and he was more company than a boat could haul.

Then this last revolution came along and the trains was cut off from Orendain[11], which is our shipping point; so we shut down all but a little development work, and it left too much time on Jimmy's hands. He took to riding out—prospecting, I thought; but I might have known. Old folks are not much company for a kid.

One day I rode over to see Moreno about some beef; and Moreno was tickled about something, which he is a proud man but jolly when he feels that way. We had two–three drinks, and he takes me by the elbow and leads me out to the main patio[12] of his house; and what do you think?

That is Moreno's hacienda you see down there in the basin. It is quite a place; white buildings, very old, and shady arches around patios with flowers and fountains and cedars trimmed into the shape of fighting cocks; green farms and cattle ranges stretching off to these blue hills, like the world with a fence around it. There was a fountain, I remember, singing a soft and lazy tune that never changed, and lazy sunshine and a warm sweet feeling that got into you. I don't know why it made me feel so cross and old.

There was Jimmy picking flowers with Moreno's daughter, and not even a servant for a chaperon!

Elena, she knew it was queer. Her face was all flushed up; why are girls prettier when they are shy? She was using a fan like these girls do, graceful, half hiding her face and laughing with those

---

10   Doña Escopeta. Lady Shotgun. Woman with an explosive personality.

11   Orendain. Possibly based on the town of Tequila, home of Orendaín Tequila, among others.

12   Patio. The inner courtyard of an hacienda, usually paved and often containing a fountain.

big brown eyes of hers; these girls can just make their eyes talk to a man. That poor kid did not know which end he was standing on.

Elena, she knew she had no business to be there with a young fellow by herself. She ducked her head and flew; but Jimmy, he comes up grinning. He had been having the time of his young life. Moreno gives him a dig in the ribs and chuckles to me, "What do you think of my young namesake, eh?"

"Namesake?" I says. I reckon I was kind of sour about it.

But it was so. Santiago is Mexican for James. Yes, and Moreno means dark colored; it is the same as Brown. Funny what a difference it makes! Santiago Moreno is a grandee, mostly Spanish and very proud; but Jimmy Brown is a plain name and a plain gringo[13] kid.

"Don[14] Santiago and I have decided," says the kid in Spanish, "that we are kin—somewhere this side of Adam."

But I would not talk Spanish to him.

"I see you are kin to Adam all right!" I says, sarcastic.

"Oh," he says, "you mean my Spanish lesson."

"Come off!" I says, snorting. "That excuse is all wore out. A walking dictionary! Why don't you think up something new?"

You can not faze that boy. He acts so innocent he is plumb impudent; solemn, you know, but his eyes just twinkles at me.

"You seem to think I am hiding something," says he.

"Not so you could notice it!" I says.

But I had to grin. You can not be sour with that boy, and how are you going to keep a young fellow from falling in love with a pretty girl? Especially if he is lonesome. I can remember when Concha looked mighty sweet to me, and she is more Indian than Elena ever thought of being. Elena is nearly white.

I can't explain. It kind of tickled me, at that—this fool kid walking right through a cast-iron custom and hardly knowing it was

---

13   Gringo. Slang term for an American, can be pejoritive.

14   Don. Lord or Mister. Masculine counterpart of Doña—Lady.

there; making up to a rich man's daughter right under her father's nose, when any other young buck would have thought he was lucky to slip a smile and a flower to her going by in her carriage! He was not trained to playing bear, which is standing on your hind legs under a girl's window and whispering for fear the old man will find it out. The only way he knew to pay attention was to march up and do it.

Riding home I tried to talk to him.

"Don't you know," I says, "they don't think it's decent for a young fellow and a girl to be together by themselves?"

"I guess," he says, cheerful, "Don Santiago knows I'm decent. At least he seems willing to take a chance."

He did not see any reason to be afraid of a girl's father. I reckon that was how he got away with it; Moreno had never seen a young fellow act so frank and ignorant, and it tickled him. He seemed to think Jimmy was quite a boy. They was all the time calling each other *tocayo*, namesake, you know, as chummy as a pair of drillers—though Moreno is one of the richest men around here.

Well, you can bust into a custom when you are ignorant, but it will sure close up on you if you stay there long enough. Once or twice I tried to talk to him.

"Son," I says, "people will say you ought to marry that girl."

"I wish they would speak to her about it!" says he, which it seems he had asked her fifteen or sixteen times already. I did not think she would do it. But that is the way these girls are; they think they have to hold off or a man will think they are cheap; but if they like him they sure know how to keep him trying.

And for a while it seemed to do him good. Even after we started shipping ore again I could not think up jobs enough to hold him; and he would come back on a high horse, joshing everybody and working like a house afire. I reckon he was used to girls, back home, and missed them.

People did talk, of course. You can not bust through cast-iron customs without making noise. Nobody said anything to me;

they knew better; but Concha was all steamed up about the women talking. And one Sunday over in Hosto, this young Felipe Cuervo, that was sweet on Elena himself, he challenged Jimmy to a duel. The first I knew about it was when the kid came home with a nick shot out of his ear. These people always shoot at your head; but Jimmy, he had shot low, like I always told him, and bust Felipe's hip for him.

I begged the kid to have some sense, but he just laughed. He was a scamp, that boy. He could be impudent in a bashful way that women like, and old folks too; he could make you laugh when you felt like kicking him in the pants. Excuse me if I talk too proud of him. He was the nearest to a son I ever had.

Drink hearty! Do you think a young fellow ought to stay away from women until he is old enough to have some sense?

Well, it would save a lot of trouble. Many a man would be alive and well that is not.

Sometimes I think the Lord never made this country for white men anyway. It is too raw. Beautiful, yes; but violent. The hills are too big and the stars come down too close. The sun is hot and the nights are cold, and when it rains it rains like hell bust loose; and something gets into you. More violent; I can't explain. You get so you do not care. You think you can take it easy, because there is plenty of time and a man lives only once.

But finally it comes to you that there will be nothing but time as long as you live; and it seems long enough, God knows.

It is all right for Indians. They do not have to think. The sun is their friend and the hills are like people to them. Time does not worry them. Take this old fellow that calls himself Guatamo—this cripple that claims to be their king. What do you think of a man with patience enough to catch a thousand humming birds?

They are not like our Indians in the United States. They are older. You would not think it to look at them, but once they had kings just like white people, and cities as big as any in the world. They built roads and bridges and pyramids, and knew things no white man knows to-day. The Spaniards never could have licked them, only they thought Spaniards was gods because they was white and had horses and guns, and they treated them friendly and let them into their cities. But the Spaniards was human, all right, and started paying attention to their women, and the trouble started—like it always does.

This old Guatamo here, he claims to be the great-great-something grandson of Guatamotzin, the prince that killed Moctezuma—or Montezuma, I expect you call him; their king, you know—to keep him from giving in to the Spaniards. And Moctezuma was his uncle, and forgave him and gave the kingdom to him when he was dying. That makes Guatamo king if it is so. He claims to know where the gold is buried, and he is crippled because he has been punished to make him tell. He has got plenty of gold, that is a sure—

Huh? Maybe he did tell them. But they never came back with any of it. They never came back at all. He is a bad man to monkey with, because the Indians think he is kind of sacred.

He does not look much like a king. Old, that is how he looks; you can not tell how old; you could believe he was Guatamotzin himself, alive—hating the Spaniards and waiting for the stars to tell him when to kill all the white men and bring back the day of the Nahuatlecas[15]—all these four hundred years.

But he is just an Indian to Moreno. I was going to tell you.

Along in this last rainy season Jimmy took to going around solemn and absent-minded, and not eating much, and after a while he tells me it is all fixed. He is going to marry Elena.

---

15   Nahuatlecas. Speakers of Nahuatl, a language group once spoken in Central Mexico by various peoples, including the Aztecs. It is still spoken today by isolated groups.

III

I TOLD him *felicidades*, happiness, you know, and he said thanks. It was none of my business; he was free, white and twenty-one[16]. He didn't have much to say about it, and I didn't.

But all of a sudden I noticed we had said it in Spanish. It seemed natural. His Spanish had got better—better than any gringo had a right to talk; his manners was better too, and it made you feel more offish and polite with him. He was not quite the same.

"Well," I says, "when does the wedding come off?"

He answers kind of vague. He says they are waiting for the legal formalities. I thought he meant the banns[17]; I did not have any idea what that kid had went and done.

But I could see he did not feel so good. I tried to get him to take a trip to the States, which it would be too late after he was mar-

---

16   Free, white and twenty-one. U.S. slang for "able to do what one wants without obtaining permission from anyone." First attested to in 1828.

17   Banns. The public announcement of an impending marriage, still practiced today in many Catholic countries and some Protestant countries. In Catholic countries, the banns must be read at mass on three successive Sundays before a marriage can be held.

ried; Elena, she has never been any farther than Guadalajara, and the States would scare her to death. I took to talking about the machinery we ought to buy, but he argues, listless, that we did not have the money to risk buying it just yet. I reckon he was not much interested in mining any more. Why should he be? Moreno owns most of this basin that is any good for farming, and he never had but this one daughter to leave it to.

Once or twice I tried to talk to him. Once I asked if him and Elena was good friends, and he thought I was joking,

"We are not getting married because we hate each other," he says, "that is a sure thing."

"I know what you are getting married for," I says. "I am not so old but what I can remember."

He was sitting just where you are sitting now, gazing out over this blue-rimmed basin that will be all his some day; and the dark was coming fast, like it is now. And by his voice I know the money and position does not mean a thing to him. He is just aching for a girl out there where little lights begin to shine, and all this lonesome twilight closing in.

This is the time when you can talk, if ever. You can not see each other's face so plain, and you forget to wonder what a man will think. The sky fading off and off, the sun just gone but burning a little while like the door of heaven that men dream about, and night and quiet spreading on the hills. You try to talk; you try to say things you can never say—like feeling in the dark to touch somebody you can hear but can not see.

He thinks it is wonderful that a girl could love him enough to marry him. A jack-leg engineer, he calls himself. He has not got any idea what a fine, upstanding, warmhearted young hellion[18] he is.

"Son," I says, "I understand all that. I was a young buck myself once, little as you would think it, and thought women was not human too. I know these girls are good at loving; it is all they know. But are you friends with her? How do you get along with

---

18   Hellion. A rowdy, mischievous person.

her, talking, and so forth? I mean—does she laugh at what you think is funny?"

I reckon I did not say it right. It kind of shut him up. By his voice I know he is just humoring me; he thinks I do not know how a young fellow feels.

Yes, him and Elena, they laugh plenty when they are together, it seems.

But I had seen them laughing, and I knew. It was not because anything was funny. It was because they were a handsome young fellow and a pretty girl.

"I mean," I says, "you will both live a long time, at least I hope so, and you will be young and high-spirited only a little while. How will you get along when you are old folks, unless you are friends and like the same kind of jokes?"

No young fellow knows how lonesome it is to be married and not understand each other's jokes. I know it does not sound like much. I tried to tell him. I could not say it any plainer than I did; but it did not sound like anything to him. He just humored me because I am an old fellow and he is young and husky. I could tell by his voice that he was just humoring me, and it made me mad because I could not make him see that being married was no joke.

After that I let him alone. It was the rainy season too, and if you are mad at anybody it is no pleasure to be cooped up with him by rain.

It was a miserable way to be. He did not half listen to anything you said, and he was all the time too polite—like a native; like Santiago Moreno, Junior. He was even polite to Concha, and she thought he was mad at her and I could not tell her different. She would fuss around doing little things for him, and she would cut her old eyes at him and wait for him to make fun of her; but he never did. It made me feel worse than if he had been downright mean to her.

Well, one night I was sitting here, the rain coming down like a wall at the edge of the porch, and all of a sudden I hear horses. These days you never know what is coming; tell you the truth, I half hoped it would be trouble. I was feeling pretty sour because me and Jimmy could not get along.

So I felt to see if my gun was loose, and give them a whoop for fear they would miss the camp. You would not want even a bandit to be lost in these hills when it is raining.

But it was two white men and a *remudero*[19] from Orendain—I bet he made them pay in advance and left the money at home—leading a pack mule loaded with suit-cases. They sure was dressy; tapered pants, and belts around their coats, and shiny boots and little silver spurs; you know, like yours; the regular tenderfoot[20] get-up. Why do tenderfeet always wear corduroy? It is hot and it soaks up water like a sponge.

One was a man about forty-five, half-drowned and completely peevish; he falls off his horse and stomps in like he is blaming me for the rain. But the other one—just a kid, fourteen or fifteen, he looks to be—acts like it is all a joke. He prances in and flops into a chair and sticks his legs up to let the water run out of his boots, grinning and wrinkling up his nose kind of cute.

"Pfuff!" says he. "I do believe it's going to rain!"

And he hops up and swings the water off his hat, and he looks younger; there is a sort of baby look about him, his black hair bushed up every way. Well, I was herding them inside when we run into Jimmy and Concha coming out to see what the commotion was; and for a minute I thought Jimmy had gone crazy. He claps his hands to his head and staggers up against the wall.

---

19   Remudero. A wrangler; an employee who takes care of the horses.
20   Tenderfoot. A newbie, an inexperienced person, especially one new to an rough area or a region.

"I am seeing things!" he moans. "I've got 'em again[21]! A flapper[22]—a real live flapper or my name is not Francis X. Bushman![23]"

"Why, Francis," says this wet kid, giggling, "how you have changed!"

And it was not a boy at all; it was a girl, for all her hair-cut and her pants like papa's. That was the only time I ever heard Concha laugh out loud.

---

21   Got 'em again. Delirium Tremens, a mental disorder from alcohol withdrawal which can cause people to see and hear things.

22   Flapper. A social movement among young women in the 1920s marked by short skirts, bobbed hair, jazz, and disdain for acceptable behavior.

23   Francis X. Bushman. One of the biggest movie stars of the 1910s and early 1920s.

The Proud Old Name

IV

HOW do you feel about a woman wearing pants? It sure does not seem right. She was around here all next day, because it kept on raining, and I could not get over being embarrassed about her legs. I could not stand to look at her hair, whacked off that way.

In this country that is what they do to a girl when she goes wrong.

But Concha, she thinks all Americans are crazy anyway, and it tickles her. She cackles right out. And Gene—that is her name, Eugenia Ward, only Gene fits her better, account of her looking and acting so much like a boy—she looks at Concha and laughs, which she seems to think Concha is funny too. She gets on some dry pants and follows Concha into the kitchen and Concha does not run her out. I hear the women just chattering in there, and I go to see if they are plaguing the girl; but it is Jimmy that is plaguing Concha and trying to make her talk English for Gene. Concha is flapping her hands and making out like she is mad, but you can tell she is tickled. It seems like old times to have Jimmy making fun of her again.

Yes, for a while he was more like himself. Him and Gene was all the time joshing each other. They seem to be talking English, but it did not make much sense. It was a circus to watch them.

"Hi, flapper!" says Jimmy, coming in from the mine.

"Don't be quaint," says Gene. "If you call me a flapper I will call you a cake eater[24] or a drug-store cowboy[25]. They went out years and years ago—two years at least."

Then Jimmy begins to limp, hitching one leg like it is wooden, and lets his hands shake and strokes where his beard could be if he had one.

"Marooned," says he in a trembly voice. "Aye, lass, well you may snicker. Poor old Ben Gunn[26] the world has passed him by. Go, child, and leave me with my memories!"

"Such as?" says Gene.

"You are too young to know," says he. "I can remember when they only showed them to the knee[27]."

"Old stuff," says Gene. "Positively mid-Victorian![28]"

"How far is it now? But stop! I shudder to think," says Jimmy, shuddering.

"They are not showing them at all," says Gene.

"Eh, well! Old ways are best," says Jimmy, very sad.

What do they care if it rains? He wraps a slicker around her and takes her over to the mine, and she takes it off and the drillers can not work for staring at her pants.

He takes Ward over, and they argue by the hour about our operations, which Ward thinks is plenty crude. Ward is a stockholder in Siete Minas, it seems; that is a big low-grade operation

---

24   Cake eater. A playboy or self-indulgent person.

25   Drug-store cowboy. A person who loafs around drugstores or on street corners, possibly dressed like a cowboy even though they are not one.

26   Ben Gunn. A character in Robert Louis Stevenson's Treasure Island who had been marooned on an island for many years.

27   Showed them to the knee. Skirts.

28   Mid-Victorian. Old-fashioned or excessively prudish.

thirty miles north of here; they are shut down because they ship bullion[29] instead of ore and it is just pie for the bandits. But the Siete Minas folks back in the States has got suspicious about getting nothing but assessments out of the mine, and sent Ward down here to investigate. Ward does not tell me this; he has got a jaw like a steel trap and all he asks is questions; but Gene, she tells Jimmy. Women have simply got to talk, and sooner or later they are bound to tell all they know.

That is the way with tenderfeet. They hear the revolution is over, and trains running again, and no Americans killed lately, and they expect profits to pick up and be as usual. They do not understand what the old-timers mean when they say a district is peaceable.

I told Ward he was a fool to go packing that girl around, and he was right upset about it.

"They told me in Guadalajara," he says, "there was no trouble in this district now."

"Depends on what you mean by trouble," I says. "If you ride by daylight, and mind your own business and give up your money peaceable if they get the drop on you, you are not likely to get shot. But a woman is different," I says. "If a daughter of mine got caught out on the trail," I says, "I would sure call it trouble."

The chances were that nothing would happen, but if a woman did run into trouble, out there in the hills, it would be too late to be sorry you had took the chance. Too many men have found out, the last ten–twelve years, that a man with a gun can make his own laws; and some of them are all right, but a good many of them are human.

So he asked me could she stay here till he got back, and I said we would be glad to have her. Yes, sir; they do say hell is full of good intentions. Ward, he did not have a bit of trouble, going or coming; but I let that girl walk right into the middle of the worst mess that has happened around here.

---

29   Bullion. Gold or silver smelted into bars or ingots, not yet coined.

Gene, she was satisfied to stay. It was early one morning when her papa rode off with this fellow from Orendain that brought him. The sun was just coming up behind the ranges; the air fresh and keen, the wet rock sparkling like a million little diamonds, the basin fading off into blue haze and all the peaks like something painted grand against the sky. A clear morning in this altitude can make you kind of drunk.

She stood here watching till they made the dip in the trail, and all of a sudden she draws a deep breath and stretches up her arms.

"Oh, all my life," she says, "I have been hungry for the hills!"

And I remember yet her gray eyes shining. That was the first time that she looked just right to me. That was the first time that I noticed freckles on her nose, and they belonged there, though her hair was nearly black.

I can't explain. She looked like something, standing there—this short-haired slim kid in her neat boots and pants, her head up and a look in her gray eyes, watching the sunrise pour across the world. Like part of it; I can't explain. Like what men think of when they hunt for gold. Boyish and brave and gay and everlasting, like what gets into men to go adventuring. It had you feeling tired and old, remembering. It had you thinking where you missed the trail when you was young.

"What is that little white place yonder?" she wants to know.

"Moreno's hacienda," says Jimmy, speaking short.

But she has read about haciendas, it seems, and she wants to know. A plantation or a ranch or something, is it? She has heard they are like ancient Spain; few—yes, feudal; that is the word she says. Barons, and so forth. Well, I have never been to Spain, but I reckon they do not have Indians for servants over there.

"Old and romantic, is it?" she wants to know.

"Old," says Jimmy, "yes. As to the romance, I am prejudiced. I am going to marry the owner's daughter."

Smiling he says it, but very sharp and clear. Gene turns to look at him and laughs. "Hot dog!" she says. "A real Spanish señorita?"

"Mexican," says Jimmy, but does not explain the difference.

"Tell me about her! Black-eyed and beautiful?"

"Brown-eyed and beautiful," says Jimmy.

"Does she speak English?"

"No."

"I should say it is romantic! Do you sing softly at midnight under her window, and did you have to fight her father and her brothers and her other lovers, like they do in books?"

She was half curious and half making fun; I reckon she did not more than half believe him; but Jimmy, he has lost his taste for joshing completely. He looks at her like he can be pushed just so far.

"Sorry to disappoint you," he says very dry and quiet; "I do not sing, softly or otherwise, at midnight or any other time. She has no brothers and her father is a very good friend of mine. I am going to take his name."

"Take his—oh!" says Gene, looking queer. "You mean—turn Mexican? I don't believe you!"

"Son," I says, "say that over again—slow!"

But he has turned his back and marched off to the mine. By the time I caught up with him he was sitting on a wheelbarrow watching the drillers in Number 3 Drift. I kind of put my hand on his shoulder, but he looked up at me so savage I thought he did not like it.

"Son," I says, "did you say you was going to change your name?"

"I did," says he, like he is not interested.

I could not get it through my head. Oh, it has been done; more than one man has took his wife's name when she is rich and his folks are nobody much. Natives, I mean; they set great store by family and name. And one way of looking at it, I reckon a girl has got as much right to her name as a man has. And yet—a man is a man. A white man is a white man, and you can not get around it.

"Why not?" says he, listless. "Moreno is a good name. It was a proud old name in Spain before Mexico was heard of—before there was any United States. It has been a great name here for a hundred years, and Don Santiago has no son to carry it on. I know how they feel about it."

But I remember how he sat there staring at that gang of drillers. They could have stood on their heads and he would not have noticed. I remember how his hands kept opening and shutting, hard, like he was feeling whether they belonged to him or Santiago Moreno, Junior. He had a fine pair of hands, husky and lean and kind of freckled on the back.

"Yes, but son," I says—"how about the way you feel?"

He makes a motion with his hands, listless; like letting go; like the natives when they mean it makes no difference.

"What is the difference?" he says. "A name—what is a name? A habit. I feel like Jim Brown; well, I shall learn to feel like Santiago Moreno."

"A habit," I says, "that you got from your pa and your grandpa and his father before him."

"It didn't mean much to them," he says, listless. "A family named Brown. Which Brown? Nobody knows."

And he tells me a little about his folks. There was not much to tell. And when you come to think of it, that is the way with most of us. Do you know who your grandpa was? Well, then, your great-grandpa? We do not bank so much on family; with us a man is more himself; and we seldom live in one place a hundred years, because we light out hunting our chance to get ahead.

Jimmy's folks had not got ahead much. His pa sold groceries and died when Jimmy was knee high to a duck, and his ma had to make dresses for a living, and she died just when he was getting big enough to be some help to her. He worked his way through school by waiting table and gathering up laundry, which it seems is no disgrace in mining school; but it is sure nothing to boast of to the Morenos.

He did not know of any near kinfolks but his grandpa, and not much about him.

"He was a carpenter," says the kid—like that.

"An honest trade enough," I says, "for Jesus Christ."

"Oh," he says, "honest," and makes that motion with his hands again, like the natives when they mean it does not amount to much. I don't know why it made me kind of mad.

"Ashamed of him, are you," I says— "Santiago?"

But it was me that was ashamed. He just looked at me.

"You asked me," he says, "and I am telling you. Elena's name means something to her; mine—is a way to know when I am spoken to."

I reckon they had been talking ancestors at him; he kept coming back to his grandpa—the only one of his he knew about.

"I don't even know what his first name was," he says. "Nobody thought it was important, not even he. A humble man; no education, never at ease in his own house; I remember he always went outdoors to smoke when my mother was there. I think he was afraid of her because she had been a school-teacher. A tired, stoop-shouldered old man with rusty shoes and a pipe, named—grandpa."

That is not much in the way of ancestors, is it? Not much to stack up against a proud old family and a girl that is in your blood like liquor. I was not blaming him; a young fellow can not think straight when he is lonesome. And yet—what if your grandpa did not get ahead? How do you know what held him back? You still have got a right to make a start and be somebody's grandpa to be proud of. You still have got a right to be yourself.

We are not proud, but we are sure as good as any Spaniard.

"Son," I says, "look here! How far has this thing gone?"

"How do you mean," he says, "how far? I have given my word. The legal end of it takes time, that's all. Time," he says, "my God! You'd think a man was going to live forever!"

And he makes a motion like throwing something away and goes charging out and gets on his horse and pours the quirt[30] to him. That is what gets you. Time. You see it coming on, day after day and every day the same, and you feel like you could not stand it. And you let yourself go to keep from thinking; do something—do anything to keep from thinking. You can do it—for a while. But you can not keep time from coming on. You get old before you learn it is no use; before you learn to sit and let the days go by. A young fellow can just eat his heart out, thinking.

I knew where he had gone. I could have guessed it, anyway, by the look in his eyes when he came in that night. Like walking in a trance; he did not even think to take his spurs off, but came in dragging them. He stops by Gene's chair—we was just eating supper—and makes her a little bow, polite and absent-minded.

"You were interested in haciendas," he says. "Don Santiago asks me to say he will be honored to have you visit his."

And he makes another little bow to Concha and says, "With permission," like a native, and sits down to eat; but he was not paying attention to anything; he was remembering. Gene, she had never seen him act like that before. You could just see her gray eyes cooling off.

"Thank you," she says, "but I'm not so interested as I was."

"As you wish," says Jimmy, too polite and vague for any use.

He did not say a word about any trouble at Moreno's. Maybe he did not know; I never got a chance to ask him, afterward. Maybe he did not talk to anybody but the family, and they are too polite to talk about the servants stealing and getting shot for it.

He just ate and went into his room and shut the door. Gene sat out here with me a while, but it was lonesome for her. I remember she tried to talk about how peaceable it was. Peaceable! Look at this basin now. These million stars that keep on shining whether you live or die; these hills that look so soft and purple-dark—they looked that way when the first Toltecs came from God knows where. They looked that way when the last Toltec

---

30　Quirt. A short, one-handed riding whip.

died on a Nahuatl altar, God knows how long ago. They looked that way when Aztec kings ruled over the empire of the Nahuatlecas; greater than Spain it was; and they looked that way when a hundred thousand Nahuatl fighting men went up against the Spaniards' guns and died. Peaceable, yes. What difference does it make to them?

I did not blame her when she went to bed. I sure was not fit company for her—old as I am and sour as I felt. What is the matter with young fellows when they get women on the brain?

The Proud Old Name

V

THAT very day Moreno had an Indian shot for stealing corn. Oh, nothing new about it; he has shot plenty of them in his time. No, he is not any kind of an officer. He does not need to be. He owns most of the land around here.

That is what all the trouble is about to-day. It is not revolution exactly; revolutions come and go, but this thing gets more so all the time. More like it is in Russia. Yes, bolshevism[31]; that is the word I mean. Francisco Madero[32], he started it here with his talk about giving the land back to the Indians. That was how he won the first revolution against Diaz[33]. And that was what finished him, too, when the Indians found out he could not do what he said.

It has been more or less the same with every revolution since, the Indians getting bolder and bolder against the rich folks. Time

---

31   Bolshevism. A far-left faction behind the communist/socialist Russian revolution of 1917.

32   Francisco Madero. 33rd president of Mexico. Instrumental in starting the Mexican Revolution of 1910.

33   Porfirio Díaz. Long-time presidential incumbent, deposed in 1911.

was when the inside walk around the plaza at Hosto was left open for a dozen fine families, but now the big hats and sandal feet and dirty blankets have crowded them out completely. They do not even dare get out of their carriages at the Sunday night concerts; they just drive around a few laps listening to the band and looking rich and proud, and then drive home complaining how the lower classes have gone crazy.

I do not know what it is coming to. It does not look possible to put things back where they was four hundred years ago. For one thing, where are you going to draw the line, when half of them have got some Spanish blood?

They have scared out a good many fine families, that is a sure thing; murdered them or run them back to Spain or to some city for protection. Moreno, though, he did not scare worth a cent. He just got prouder and prouder. He went ahead and had this Indian shot for stealing corn, and the very next day he had a woman—

Huh? Well, not exactly. They just catch a man stealing and start off to jail with him and shoot him trying to escape—you know. The law of flight, they call it. I am not saying it is wrong, A rich man has to protect his property, and he can not be riding around to trials all the time. It sounds kind of rough, but it does discourage stealing, that is a sure thing.

Anyway, it is the way this country has been run four hundred years. But the rich men are mostly Spanish and the thieves are mostly Indian, and you can not blame the Indians for getting tired of it.

We did not know a thing about it here. I was sitting here next morning when Jimmy came out, and I reckon he did not sleep much; his eyes looked like burnt holes in a blanket, and he did not say good morning or be durned to you; he just sat down. Then Gene came out and he got up stiff as a ramrod.

Gene, she went right up to him and put her hand on his arm.

"Jimmy," she says, "I didn't mean to be impertinent. I guess it didn't seem quite real to me. It's—it's all so wide and new," she says, "out here, I don't feel so darned real myself."

"It's quite all right," says Jimmy—polite if it kills him.

"It's not all right," says Gene. "I mean well, but there's simply nobody home. I feel like an oil can[34]," she says, "making wise cracks about things I don't know anything about. Broad A me[35]," she says. "It's just what I deserve."

I know it does not make sense. But it would take a wooden man to be mad at her when she looks like that, her gray eyes looking up at him so honest—sober and sorry, like a kid. Jimmy, he kind of gulps and pats her hand.

"You're all right," he says. "I'm the oil can. Go on," he says, "ask me. Ask me anything; ask me about any of the fourteen men I have killed —or is it sixteen?" And he hauls his gun out of the holster and pretends to be counting the notches in the butt, which there is not any. "Seventeen," he tells her, solemn.

"That is the boy!" says Gene, and I will be eternally dad-gummed if she did not stand up on her tiptoes and offer to kiss him. I never saw such a girl.

Jimmy, he did not do it. He was so embarrassed he turned kind of pale, which he did not feel good that morning anyway.

"Get away from me, woman! You are shocking the assembled multitude," he says, which I did feel kind of like a multitude, at that—kissing and going on; though you could tell she did not mean a bit of harm. "Necking and hitting in the clinches[36] is barred," he says, whatever that means; I never did find out, because Concha came and said breakfast was ready.

But it was more cheerful to see them joshing each other. It was a real pretty morning, and first thing I knew they were talking about riding over to Moreno's after all.

------

34   Feel like an oil can. Possibly an impostor.

35   Broad A me. Possibly, to snub or speak with disdain, as though using the British Received Pronunciation.

36   Necking and hitting in the clinches. Necking is kissing or making out; clinch is a boxing term that refers to boxers temporarily 'hugging' each other. It is generally frowned upon to hit in the clinch.

Well, sir, I did not have the heart to interfere. I did not think they would run into any trouble; it's only nine kilometers and the trail is wide open all the way.

But I knew what they wanted with her over there. They would not be easy till they got a look at her. These women think every woman in the world is trying to steal their man.

Well, it would not hurt them to be shocked a little, and Gene was plumb tickled about going exploring. Jimmy, he tells her about their medieval hospitality.

"The man at the gate will kiss your hand," he says; "ancient-retainer[37] stuff, you know; and Don Santiago will tell you his house is yours, and make you believe it too."

"Hot dog!" says Gene. "I'm crazy about ancient retainers. We had a butler once that stayed with us six months."

That is the way she talks. Hot dog or the bee's hips or the snake's elbows means she is tickled. When she says she is crazy she does not mean she is crazy, she means she likes a thing.

"I can rake up a side-saddle[38]," says Jimmy. "Our storekeeper's wife has got one somewhere. Have you got a female skirt?"

"Of course," says Gene, "but what's the big idea? I can't ride side-saddle. I saw a picture of one once; prehistoric, you know. Everybody rides cross-saddle now."

"Not here!" says Jimmy, very dry and final.

Short hair was scandalous enough, without bringing in a woman in pants and straddle of a horse. The Morenos would have fell dead.

I knew what they would think, anyway, about a girl riding nine kilometers with a young fellow, and nobody else along. They would think it was not decent. Besides, I felt responsible for Gene. Not that Jimmy couldn't take care of her; he is a nervy

---

37   Ancient retainer. An old person in the service of a lord.

38   Side-saddle. A horse saddle that positions both of a woman's legs on one side. It was once considered indecent for a woman to ride astraddle, with a leg on each side.

kid and handy with a gun; but there is no use talking, two men is twice as good as one in case of trouble.

So I said I was about due to ride over and see Moreno myself. Gene came dancing out with a dress on, pretty but not a riding habit by any means, and a blue hat like something wrapped around her head. Well, sir, you would be surprised. She looked real grown up. But she sure did not act it. She was like a monkey about that side-saddle, which she had on silk stockings and her dress was pretty but not long.

Dresses do make a woman look different and you can not get around it. More precious somehow. I remember thinking I could not stand to look her papa in the eye if anything was to happen to that girl.

It felt peaceable enough—a pretty morning, the basin spread out like a bright green checkerboard, the horses clipping along and these two kids joshing each other. Jimmy, he was lying when he told her he did not sing. He can sing fine. You can hear him half a mile when he feels good. Riding along, he busts out, and pretty soon Gene joins in. It did not make much sense—about yes, we have not got any bananas[39], and throwing the dishes away instead of washing them[40]; but it made you feel right gay, at that.

Gene, she could sing rings around him. Her voice goes weaving in and out through his; not like the *segundo*[41] that the native women sing; *segundo* sounds wild and sad, but this was more like joking with the tune.

"Hot dog!" says Jimmy. "The barber-shop[42] kid!"

---

39   Yes, we have not got any bananas. "Yes, We Have No Bananas," novelty song by Frank Silver and Irving Cohn, 1923.

40   Throwing the dishes away instead of washing them. Sorry, not a clue. If you know what this is, please e-mail me and let me know. Thanks!

41   Segundo. A close harmony generally lower than the melody, popular in Latino music of the 19th century.

42   Barber-shop. Barbershop quartet music, an American-style a cappella close harmony.

Gene, she just laughed. She was not a bit touchy about her hair being cut.

They get to singing softer and slower, riding along. Jimmy rides up close and puts his head down by hers, and sings with his eyes half shut like he was listening; and it was worth listening to. It kind of gave you a feeling up the back, the way her voice slid over his like a bow on soft deep fiddle strings.

"That is the boy!" says Jimmy, and he turns around and asks me, "How's that for close harmony, huh?"

"It's right harmonious," I says, "but maybe you could get closer if you was to climb on to the same horse," I says, sarcastic, which Gene did not look much like a boy that day—her face pink with the wind, and this blue hat kind of cute around it, and her eyes bright with singing. I remember how pretty her mouth looked, changing to let her voice float high and clear or settle to a whisper like the far-off hum of bees.

"Here's an old one," she says, and croons a piece of a tune to him and asks him if he knows it, "but full of dirty swipes[43]."

That was what she said—dirty swipes; but there was nothing dirty about it. It is a real sweet song. I have heard Jimmy sing it many a time.

Oh, come, my love, and walk with me—

That is the way it starts, all on one note, only her voice chimes different on every word. Then it drifts into singing gentle and slow. I edged my horse off on to the grass to keep his hoofs from rattling. Their voices melting in together; gentle and sad and sweet, like a slow wind and rain on the roof and thinking of old times when you lie awake at night. I don't remember all of it, only at the end it is something about

—sever,

Say you will leave me never,

---

43   Dirty swipes. In barbershop quartet music, "snakes" and "swipes" refer to the technique of altering a chord by a changing one or more non-melodic voices.

Say you'll be mine—forever,

For I—

I can't explain. I used to sing pretty good, but it has been a long time since I tried it. His voice goes fading up and fading down and hers comes melting into it, golden-soft.

"I love… but you."

I did not know the boy could sing so sweet. But I reckon he noticed he was riding too close to her and felt kind of embarrassed about it. He let go her arm and rode along not saying anything. He hardly said another word all the way to the hacienda.

Maybe you noticed before it got dark, there is a kind of a crack out there across the basin? It does not look like much from here, but it is deep and there is quite a river in it. The ford is just outside the hacienda. Riding down to it I see four–five old men sitting there; not doing anything; just sitting there. Yes, everything seemed to be quiet. Too quiet; I can see it now. I remember my left elbow kind of aching where I was shot once, and I thought it was going to rain. But I reckon it was the feel of trouble in my bones.

And I remember how quick old Tolo jumped up from his chair by the big gate where he has been sitting thirty or forty years. Like he was looking for somebody or something; I did not think of it at the time. It looked peaceable enough, the dogs running out to bark and the little naked kids sidling up to stare at Gene, which they had never seen a woman with a hat on.

Tolo unbuckles our spurs and says we are welcome to our house; that is the custom; it does not mean a thing.

"Ancient retainer?" says Gene.

"As advertised," says Jimmy, speaking short. It does beat all how a young fellow can go from sour to gay and back again.

Of course Tolo is not a butler or anything; just a *portero*[44], a wrinkled old peon[45] with dusty sandals and baggy cotton clothes;

---

44   Portero. Gatekeeper.

45   Peon. In that period of Mexican history, a person held in compulsory servitude; a menial worker or drudge.

but he is plenty ancient. And there is something about a place like that. There is a feeling, and you can not get around it. Out there in the middle of the basin, green fields and cattle ranges stretching off to these blue hills; these long white walls from the days when every hacienda was a fort; these cobbled courtyards worn by horses riding in and out a hundred years—you can not realize that it will ever change. It feels solid, settled, the stones and the houses and the people; and what they do seems right because they have been doing it so long. You could see how it had crept into Jimmy. You could see it creeping into Gene. Tolo bows down and kisses the back of her riding glove, and she was all fixed to laugh, but all of a sudden a queer look comes in her eyes.

"Quick, Jimmy," she whispers, "tell me what I do! I thought it would be funny, but it isn't. It's—dignified!"

Yes, it is kind of touching—these faithful old servants being so humble to you, and all. But it is no more natural for them to be servants than it is for you or me. Once they was proud, too, and made slaves out of people they had beat in fighting.

No, sir, white men do not know it all. Concha can tell you things that happened when the white race was a pup. She did not read it in a book; the Nahuatlecas do not have books nowadays; the Spaniards burned them all. But you can not keep people from telling their children. It is like looking down a long, dim, splendid hall into the centuries. You get a hazy glimpse of what they used to be—what they are yet, inside, and always will be. Splendid and pitiful; I can't explain. Patient and pitiful, waiting for the stars to tell them when their day will come again.

Maybe it will. Who knows? They are sure getting bolder. It seems Guatamo had sent word to Moreno about mistreating Indians, but you can imagine how much attention Moreno paid to it.

Guatamo is the one that claims to be their king. Myself, I always thought he was just a yarn the mothers told their children. Concha got it from her mother when she was a baby, and she is forty or fifty now. Huh? Yes, I know she looks older than that. These women are grown at fourteen and start getting old at twenty-five.

That was why Elena is kind of touchy about her age; I was going to tell you. Elena is nineteen, which is pretty old not to be married yet.

Guatamo, he claims to be descended from Guatamotzin—the tzin Guatamo, that killed his own uncle Moctezuma, because the Spaniards was getting him all fuddled with Christianity. It may be so; I do not claim to know. I reckon he is kind of cracked. He can sit still so long you would not swear he is alive, only his eyes—black and alive with hate that never changes. Pitiful too. He does not understand the white man's world. Gold is no good to him. Time does not mean a thing to him. How long do you think it takes to catch a thousand humming birds? Not just the common gray ones, either; the colored ones, like little jewels dancing in air; *huitzin*[46], they call them, because they are sacred to their god Huitzil[47]. Many a Spaniard has been sacri—

Eh?

Oh! *Eres tu*[48], Concha?

'Sta bien. Ahorita vamos[49]. She says our chocolate is ready.

I wonder how long she has been listening there. Did I say anything about Jimmy's grandpa? It is a kind of a joke, but you could never make her see it. I will have to tell you afterward. You can not get her to talk English, but she listens and you never know how much she gets.

---

46   Huitzin. Nahuatl word for 'hummingbird.'

47   Huitzil. Huitzilopochtli, Aztec god of sun, war, and human sacrifice.

48   Eres tu? Is that you?

49   'Sta bien. Ahorita vamos. Okay, we're coming.

The Proud Old Name

VI

YOU noticed, Concha would not sit down with us at supper? She is afraid you would not think she is good enough. That is the way the Spaniards have made them feel. Lower classes, that is what they call the Indians. *Pelados*; peeled ones; that is why upper-class Mexicans wear all the whiskers they can raise, to prove they have not got much Indian blood. Moreno, he is as proud of his beard as he is of his old Spanish name. He is high class; I was going to tell you. He knows better than to get haughty with me, but he would think Concha was a servant even if she had a million dollars.

Where did I leave off? Oh, yes; about Guatamo—this crippled old Aztec that claims to be their king.

Well, while Jimmy was having this quarrel with Moreno I hear people running in the patio, and I— Huh? I thought I told you. It was about this servant spilling a plate of *mole* in Gene's lap. Huh? Why, *mole* is turkey cooked in a black gravy of ground-up peppers. It is real tasty, but nothing for a tenderfoot to tackle. It will knock your head off if you are not used to it.

Where did I leave off anyway?

No, sir, Gene did not feel like laughing any more. There is no use talking, there is something about a place where the same people have lived for generations. These echoing courtyards and these solemn brown women peeping out of doors, quiet—I remember how loud a *vaquero's*[50] spurs sounded leading our horses away. The dark *zaguán*[51] of Moreno's house, the iron-barred *cancel*[52] grinding open to let us into the patio—quiet; so quiet that it scared up the pigeons around the fountain. And the servant says will we have the goodness to be seated while he tells the master, and Gene sat there looking at these thick old arches and the heavy purple clouds of bougainvillea and the cedars all trimmed into shapes. Lost, that was how she looked; little and quiet and young.

Moreno, he did not make her feel at home. He looks kind of fierce when he is not jolly. He is real dark-complected and his eyes make her nervous about her legs, which her dress was modest enough when you got used to it, but certainly not long. Oh, he was polite; they always are; he smiles—that is, he shows his teeth through his beard—and bows very low; too low; there was something sarcastic about it—and says he is her servant; just introducing himself; not that Santiago Moreno is anybody's servant. Not so, Bolivia!

Why are customs stricter about women? When Jimmy used to be ignorant he could just laugh it off; but they sure did not make any allowances for Gene. They looked cross-eyed about her hat until she got nervous about it and took it off to see what was the matter with it, and you ought to have seen them lift their eyebrows about her hair being cut. In this country it means a girl has been disgraced.

Moreno takes us into the *sala*[53], stiff like a funeral with heavy curtains and pictures of saints and ancestors and about twenty chairs set straight around the wall, and there we sat. Myself, I do

---

50   Vaquero. A Mexican cowboy.

51   Zaguán. A passageway from front door of an hacienda to the central patio.

52   Cancel. A door or gate made of iron bars.

53   Sala. Main hall or parlor used for receiving guests.

not like to sit in *salas*. Out in the *corredor*[54] is good enough for me, where you can get some air and watch the pigeons in the patio. But Gene was a stranger and they had to treat her dignified. Polite, that is the way they are; even if they feel like poisoning you.

It got on Gene's nerves too. She jumped when Moreno clapped his hands to tell a servant to bring wine.

Jimmy, he was no help to her. He translates what she says, polite—like a native; like Santiago Moreno, Junior. I could not help thinking how he had changed since the first time I saw him in this house. He was not jolly with Moreno any more; he was respectful; that is the way native young bucks are raised to treat their father, like he was the Almighty or something. It made you kind of sick. Of course it was none of my business. I was only his partner and he was going to be Moreno's son.

You ought to have seen Gene's face when they hugged each other. Myself, I never give the *abrazo*[55] if I can help it. I can not see any sense to hugging a full-grown man.

Well, old lady Moreno comes in—she is short and fat and powdered heavy because they like to look as white as they can—and she does not talk because she does not know anything to say. She just sits. And Gene gets more nervous trying not to notice the powder and perfume, and the senora is plumb flabbergasted about Gene's hat and legs. These women do not wear hats; they will wear a mantilla[56] worth five hundred dollars, but they think hats are sinful vanity. You never see them outside of cities. And you would think they did not have any legs, they wear so many petticoats. They think legs are not modest.

Elena sails in, and she sure had her war paint on. I do not mean paint or powder; she did not need much because she is fairly white anyway, and mad. She floats up to Gene and bows and

---

54   Corredor. Corridor or hallway. In this case, likely the zaguán.

55   Abrazo. A hug, sometimes including a cheek kiss, which is a standard greeting in many parts of Latin America.

56   Mantilla. A veil or shawl made of lace or silk worn over the head and shoulders.

says, "Elena Moreno, your servant, Señorita," very polite, but her big brown eyes look more like "What is this the cat dragged in?"

Gene did not know enough to say her own name; Jimmy had to do it for her. She was so flustered that she stood up to shake hands, and it makes Elena madder because it means Gene is younger.

I reckon women are natural enemies about men. They do not trust any man with any woman under forty; they seem to think a man is plumb helpless if a woman gets after him. Yes, sir, Elena was going to show Jimmy that no shameless American girl could be prettier than she was. She sits down by her mama and folds her hands and lets her pretty head droop graceful and sorrowful, and starts talking to him out of the corner of her eyes; and I have got to admit that she did throw Gene in the shade. Elena is sure a pretty girl—these silk skirts sweeping out from her little waist, and this high graceful comb in her hair, her pretty mouth peeping out from behind her fan and her shoulders so round and smooth; they think it is all right to show the upper part of them.

Gene does not talk with her eyes; they are too straight and honest. They only show how she feels, which is that she has lost her taste for haciendas. She leans over and asks me if it is about time to beat it—meaning go home. That is the way she talks.

But of course we could not do that. You can not ride in and out of an hacienda after riding nine kilometers to get there. They would have thought we was *informal*, which is a whole lot worse than informal in English. In Spanish it means you do not care for anybody's feelings, or keep your word, or know how to act proper.

"Gene," I says, "you play the piano, don't you? Anybody that can sing like you can must play the piano. Play us a piece."

"Piano?" she says, looking around for it. She did not know it was a piano, which it is an old one, little and squarish. She got real excited about it, asking how old it was and cooing to it and touching the keys like she was afraid it would fall to pieces.

But they did not know how old it was. I reckon it had always belonged to the Morenos.

"The señorita likes it?" says Moreno, and Jimmy translates.

"I'm crazy about it!" says Gene.

"She likes it very much," says Jimmy.

"Then it is hers," says Moreno.

Polite, that is the way they are; they will offer you anything you admire; and they may think you are crazy, but they will not back out if you have got the nerve to take it. Gene, she joked a little about carrying it home under her arm, but Jimmy did not think it was funny to make fun of customs. No, sir, he was a different boy.

It had a queer tone, thin but fairly sweet. She played something real soft and solemn, like being respectful to it; and the Morenos clapped their hands, polite.

Jimmy, he did not hardly hear it. Elena, she was sure talking with her eyes. These girls can talk to a man by the hour and never say a word; yes, sir, I am not so old but what I can remember. It is enough to make a young fellow dizzy.

But all of a sudden he looks round at Gene. She was playing something different; I bet that old piano never made a noise like that before. Not loud, but kind of sly and cute; it tickled you; I can't explain. It kind of made your feet jiggle. Jimmy, he fidgets for a minute and then goes over by her and starts singing to himself.

"I'll be round to get you in the taxes, honey—[57]"

Something like that; whatever it means, getting you in the taxes. And about dancing the two-step, and something about jolly roll blues[58]. I ask you now!

Well, that was all right, though the Morenos did not like him to be singing English, because they do not know what it is about. But all of a sudden he kind of holds out his elbows and wiggles

---

57   "I'll be down to get you in a taxi, Honey," Lyrics of "Darktown Strutters'
     Ball" by Shelton Brooks, 1917

58   Jolly Roll Blues. A mis-heard reference to Jelly Roll Morton's "Jelly Roll
     Blues," 1915, mentioned in the lyrics of "Darktown Strutters' Ball."

his shoulders—you know. I pretty near fell dead. It is a motion you can not make before a lady, let alone three of them.

"Santiago!" says Moreno, roaring at him. "Hast thou no shame?"

Gene was so surprised she stopped playing. She was not shocked or anything; I reckon she did not see him do it.

"What's all the shootin' for?" she says. "Are we in wrong?"

She did not mean shooting; at least I did not hear any. Not then.

"I pulled a little shimmy[59]," says the kid, sheepish.

"Why not?" says Gene.

I ask you now! Of course he had not pulled anybody's shimmy; but it is not even polite to talk about. She looks around, innocent, and she sees the way the Morenos are looking. Well, sir, I did not know what to do. I was not brought up in a parlor with three ladies, all mad.

"Don Santiago," I says, "the señorita has never seen an hacienda. Have you the goodness to escort her that she may view the gardens and the stables?"

That is the way with Spanish; you talk polite, no matter how sour you feel. It would have been ridiculous if it had not been so miserable—this fool kid acting polite half the time and natural the other half. It was no pleasure being there. But they have got certain ways of doing, and that is all there is to it. They would have thought we was rude to go home before dinner. They got into the habit of feeding visitors in the days when settlements was few and far between, and they will do it yet or die.

I did not see any sign of trouble. Maybe the peons and *vaqueros* was extra quiet when we came around; I was feeling pretty sour and I did not notice. Maybe Moreno was extra proud with them; he would be; that is the way he is. You can not scare him. He has been a big man here too long.

---

59   Shimmy. A dance move in which the shoulders are shaken back and forth. Uncle Lew has apparently mistaken "shimmy" for "chemise," an intimate woman's undergarment.

Nobody told us about this peon being shot the day before for stealing corn. I would not have thought a thing about it anyway. You have to have servants to work a place like that, and you have to be boss or get out. I am not blaming Moreno; he treated them the only way he knew. That is the way the Spaniards have always treated them, making them build churches and be Christians, and flogging them for the good of their souls. Nobody told us about him being warned.

Gene, she thought the gardens were beautiful, which they are, and she liked the horses, which Moreno has certainly got some fine ones. She talked baby talk to Moreno's prize bull for being so old and fat and sulky; she wanted to go in his stall and pet him. She would not believe us when we told her that bull had killed four men. She thought we was joshing her, like Jimmy did about the notches in his gun. That is the way with girls; they are raised peaceable and they do not realize. The wonder is that they are so spunky when hell begins to pop.

The Proud Old Name

VII

WELL, sir, I know it is not polite to talk English and then laugh; but what is the use of being miserable when you can find some little thing that is funny? I am not blaming Elena for being mad. It must have been a strain to sit by Gene and be polite to her when she felt like choking her; high-strung, that is the way she is; and Jimmy, he hardly noticed Elena all during dinner. Him and me got tickled about Gene.

Gene, she did not know the name of anything she ate, but she was going to be polite or bust. She was a wonder, that kid. She is not very big and you know how native dinners are; thin soup and then thick soup and then *fideos*[60]; venison and then beef and then turkey *mole*, all with more vegetables than you can shake a stick at, topped off with beans and dessert and coffee and wine. And every time she stops eating, Moreno, he says, polite, that he is afraid she does not like it, and Jimmy translates and she eats it to be polite.

---

60   Fideos. Noodles; in this case probably a chicken-noodle soup.

She did not know you are supposed to say it is delicious but you have not got any appetite. And we did not tell her. It was a low-down trick; but we got tickled, watching her.

"Five dollars she makes it and lives!" I says to Jimmy, nudging him in the ribs and whispering, which of course we was sitting on one side of the table and the girls on the other.

He took the bet. I admit it did not look possible, but I still believe I would have won if it had not been for the turkey *mole*. She took a good big bite of it to get it over with, which very likely she could not taste anything by that time anyway. But *mole* is something else again for a tenderfoot. It is not just peppery; it is like eating dynamite if you are not used to it.

"I am afraid the señorita does not like the *mole*," says Moreno, being polite, and Jimmy kicks my shin and translates as solemn as a judge. Not that he is cruel by nature; he was more used to pepper and he did not realize.

"Tell him I'm crazy about it," says Gene, gasping for breath and drinking water and clapping her napkin to her mouth and trying manful not to cry. "Tell him anything, but give me air!"

"Don't you eat it, kid!" I says. "You have made a good game try and it is worth the money."

But Jimmy, he sees the tears running down her face and feels like a low-down pup because he has let her suffer.

"I ought to be hung!" he says, and starts to explain it to Moreno. "She is crazy—that is, she loves—that is, I mean—"

You can not think in English and talk Spanish. It does not come out right. He used the wrong word for loves; he even used the wrong word for hot; he meant peppery, *picante*; but he was so sorry for Gene that he did not hardly know what he was saying.

"I mean," he says, stuttering, "she is not crazy, she only says she is crazy—I mean she says she is not crazy—"

I reckon the Morenos thought we was all crazy. The *mole* did not taste hot to them.

"Papa," says Elena, "with permission—I can not—"

She was plumb white and her voice was trembling. She makes a motion with both hands and jumps up to leave the table, and she bumped right into the servant just as the woman was reaching for Gene's plate; and flop goes turkey and black gravy and all into Gene's lap.

That finished Gene. Elena, she was plumb paralyzed. A thing like that is just terrible to a native; they are so proud, they know how mortified they would feel if it was to happen to them when they was company, and they are just speechless to have such a thing happen in their house. But Gene, she had been polite all she could stand. She went limp in her chair and fairly whooped and laughed.

"Tell them it doesn't matter," she gasps, waving her hands like she could not get her breath. "Tell them it's all right. I'm all right. Everything's all right. Jimmy, for the love of Mike, get me out of here before I go into hysterics!"

But she was already in them. It sure did not help matters any. The Morenos, they do not laugh when they are mortified; all they could figure was that she was laughing at them or their dinner or their servant being clumsy. No, sir, it was not dignified—Jimmy running around and shaking her and begging her is she burnt or anything, and Moreno and his wife standing up to apologize, and the servant down on her knees trying to scrape the stuff out of Gene's lap. Poor Gene just laughed harder than ever.

No, sir, they do not laugh things off. They just get fighting mad; and all they know to do is blame the servant. Of course the woman was scared to talk back. She just stood and took it all like a dumb animal caught out in a storm.

So I touched Elena on the shoulder and told her to tell them it was her fault, bumping into the woman that way. Well, sir, she whirled on me like a tiger.

"You!" she says. "Who are you that you should come into this house and laugh? Who are you that you should accuse me in defense of a miserable *india*? You—the husband of one! But naturally!"

She read my funeral proper. I am not blaming her; high-strung, that is the way she is; and she was upset plenty, Jimmy paying attention to another girl and petting her and trying to make her stop laughing. Besides, what is the use of getting mad at a woman? All you can do is talk, and they can outtalk you every time. And it is so that Concha is an Indian. What is the use of getting mad about it?

"Gene," I says, "if you think you can walk now, let's be going. I reckon our company can be spared."

But Jimmy, he turns around and catches Elena by the arm.

"Be quiet!" he says, speaking quiet himself.

She tries to jerk loose, but is not strong enough. And you can tell she is glad she is not. It is a relief to her to turn loose and fight; she is Indian enough herself to want to be treated rough.

"You!" she screams at him—not calling him thou. "Who are you to reproach me? You, who have brought this shameless woman into my house!"

But of course fighting is not dignified. Jimmy, he was not hurting her; only trying to make her listen to him; but Moreno bawls at him.

"Santiago! Blockhead boy! Art thou crazy?"

Then Jimmy forgot himself. He give that girl a shake she would remember. Her head pretty near bobbed off and her comb went spinning across the floor. It was the surprise of her young life. He turned her loose and she stood there like a lamb.

"Almost!" he says, breathing hard but speaking quiet. "Am I to tolerate that my friends shall be insulted in this house? You knew the señorita was a foreigner when you asked me to bring her here, yet you have dared to look her from above to below because her customs are not the customs of the country. You dare—"

"Silence!" bawls Moreno. I reckon he could not believe his ears. "Is it thus that a son shall address a father? Is it that I shall teach thee?"

There was a minute when he looked like murder. By gum, I wish you had been there. This half-freckled, blue-eyed young son-of-a-gun standing up to Santiago Moreno and calling him down in his own house; speaking quiet but looking that fellow square in the eye.

"I am not your son," he says. "I keep my word; but I was born a foreigner and I can not remake myself in a day. I am not a child that you should humiliate me. Lay hand on me and you will see. I keep my word," he says, "but I do not tolerate that my friends shall be treated so. Elena has dared to reproach Don Luis with his wife that is an Indian. Is it that she feels shame for the Indian blood in her own veins?"

"And who are you," Elena blazes at him, "that you should dare to tell me what I dare?"

She was just aching to be treated rough—her eyes just blazing at him, daring him, her head up and her hair half down; right wild and beautiful; I can't explain. But Jimmy, he did not touch her. There was a minute when you could hear them breathing. That was when I heard people running in the patio. I remembered it afterward; I remember kind of wondering what their hurry was.

Jimmy, he makes a motion with his hands like letting go.

"Say I am nobody," he says, quiet. "Call it that. Nevertheless he is my friend. You shall unblame yourself to him."

"And if I do not?" says Elena, panting.

"I go," he says, "with God."

That is a way of saying go and not come back—never, *jamás*[61], not any more forever! I grabbed him by the arm.

"Well, come on, son!" I says. "Let's go!"

But you do not know that kid. Not so, Bolivia! He had give his word and he was giving them a chance to hold him to it if they wanted.

A mule is wishy-washy compared to him when he gets it into his head a thing is right. And I won't deny there had been talk about him courting Elena right in the house that way—going to

---

61   Jamás. Never.

see her, American fashion. She would have a hard time finding another husband around here.

I am not saying Moreno thought of that. Maybe he did; or maybe it hit his Spanish pride just right.

"*Eso*[62]!" he roars, "That is the way, my Santiaguito[63]! Thou art indeed my son! A Moreno is loyal. A Moreno does not tolerate!"

And he throws his arms around the kid, patting him on the back and calling him his little Santiago and making a fuss over him. It was enough to make you sick, which Jimmy is as big as Moreno ever thought of being. And he roars to Elena, jovial, that she has got to apologize to me and Gene, and she does it. That is, she says she is sorry and I said it was all right; not that she cared; she did not hardly look at me; she was looking at Jimmy. That is the way with proud folks, they get tame awful quick if you are prouder.

"Thou are not angry with me any more?" she whispers to him.

And he smiles to her; but he was kind of quiet and pale; listless; I can't explain.

"No," he says, "I am not angry with thee, Elena. I know it was because thou didst not understand."

Nor never would. I did not have the heart to hang around any more, and Gene's dress being ruined was a good excuse. I says with permission I will take her home. Jimmy, he says with permission he will accompany us, and the señora says we have permission, and we shook hands all round and said much pleasure, all very quiet and polite. And Moreno clapped his hands to tell the servant to tell the *corralero*[64] to have our horses saddled.

The servant did not come. Nobody came. Moreno steps out into the patio and roars for somebody to send somebody quick. The pigeons flew up and settled down and that was all. The house was silent as the grave.

---

62 Eso! That's the way!

63 Santiaguito. Little Santiago; Jimmy.

64 Corralero. The worker in charge of the horses in a corral.

That was when I remembered people running in the patio. I says maybe something has happened; but we went outside and could not see a soul. We got clear round the chapel before we see the *administrador*[65] coming from the outer gate. He looks at Moreno and jerks a thumb over his shoulder, half sarcastic and half joshing and half upset about it too.

"Our friend the king," he says, "in his own person."

Moreno swears and grabs a machete off a saddled horse and goes stomping out the gate. King or no king, he would not stand for any foolishness from any Indian.

---

65   Administrador. Manager, administrator.

The Proud Old Name

VIII

THIS was the only time I ever saw Guatamo. Mighty few white men have. He does not get around much; he can not walk much and he will not ride a horse because the Spaniards brought them. That was what those old men had been doing down there by the ford all morning—waiting for him. Don't ask me how they knew that he was coming. How do Indians know anything? Don't ask me what he thought he was going to do about Moreno treating peons the way he did. I reckon the poor old gump[66] did not have any more idea than a goat. Myself, I think he is kind of cracked; but it is bad business fooling with anything that a million mothers tell their children.

Myself, I do not swear he is a king. He has got gold ornaments that was never made in these days—plenty of them; they say it is the gold of Moctezuma; but he may be just a crazy old fellow that has stumbled on it and has fooled himself into believing he is descended from Guatamotzin by thinking about it fifty or a hundred years. That is how he got crippled, trying to make him tell where the gold is. The fellows that done it, they never lived

---

66   Gump. Slang term for a foolish or dull-witted person.

to brag about it, though. These Indians are used to being kicked around themselves, but Guatamo is like Jesus Christ to them.

I would not let Jimmy and Gene go down. It was none of our business to be mixing in.

Outside the gate the ground falls away sharp down to the river. It was like a high seat at a bull ring—looking down on this crowd of peons and women and children, the big straw hats of *vaqueros* tossing here and there like chips on a pond—surging back out of Moreno's way. No, sir, Moreno was not afraid of any quantity of Indians. I remember the dust spurting under his feet, tramping down solid and savage. I remember the whacks he gave them with the flat of the machete when they did not move fast enough.

"Like slaves!" says Jimmy, breathing through his nose.

They are not slaves, of course. They are supposed to get wages; the way it works, though, is that they get credit for clothes and food, and so forth, and the master takes it out of the wages and the wages never catch up and so they can not quit. That is the old system; they are trying to do away with it, but as long as there is rich men in this country there will be peonage. They get along pretty good, at that. Only when something like this comes up you feel right sorry for them.

There was twenty or thirty little naked kids down there on their little naked knees getting Guatamo's blessing. You ought to have heard them yell when Moreno whacked their little naked behinds. Likely it was the first time he had ever noticed them, and it scared them half to death.

One of the old men holds up his right hand, solemn, and says something. It was too far to hear; but I heard Moreno bellowing all right.

"What king nor what nothing! Hola! Sebastian! Gonzalo! Pepe! Drive me these cattle to their stalls! I finish with this foolishness. I show them that in this *barrio*[67] there is no king but me."

---

67   Barrio. Neighborhood.

Roaring to his *sobrestantes*[68], his overseers, you know; proud men themselves and used to making peons step.

"Oh! Oh!" says Gene. "What is the matter? What are they fighting for?"

You could not call it fighting. Cattle he called them, and cattle they acted like. That is the difference between hacienda peons and drillers or muckers[69] in a mine. They are not free labor, used to going where they can get the best wages. They was born working for Moreno; it is a habit with them to be afraid of him and the *sobrestantes*. When they are hit they move; the *sobrestantes* yelling and kicking them right and left, Moreno roaring and laying on with the machete. I reckon he did not care much whether he hit them with the flat or the edge. Some of them was bleeding pretty bad, stampeding past us up the hill. Naked kids crying and stumbling around like scared rabbits, and scared mothers screaming at them to run faster.

It was not pretty to watch; but we did not run. There was nowhere to run to but where the stampede was going. I just pulled Gene to one side out of the dust and waited.

Moreno comes up to us, puffing and blowing but very polite.

"Señorita," he says, "most deeply I regret if this impertinence has distressed your grace. Forgive one more moment of delay and I send your horses to you."

Then he grins and points with the machete.

"Behold," he says, "the king and all his court!"

He had not hit Guatamo or the old men; maybe it came to him that he had better not. Guatamo sitting down there by the river, only these three or four worn-out old peons left to do him honor. Only these two ignorant, half-naked young hill Indians squatting there like statues with their paddles in their hands; only the water rippling past his painted canoe like it has rippled for ten thousand years, not caring. Gene had to go down and get a look at him. But he did not give any sign of seeing us—this poor old king

68   Sobrestantes. Overseers; foremen.
69   Muckers. A worker who removes dirt and waste.

of slaves; this shriveled relic of a forgotten empire, sitting there, so still you could not swear he was alive, his crazy black eyes staring straight at Gene Ward and never flickering. Maybe he did not see. Maybe the white man's world goes on around him like a dream.

"Oh, lovely! Lovely!" says Gene. "But what is it? Velvet?"

She meant the cape that covered his old bones. Color—a million colors melted into one; color that shimmered and flowed when you moved, like silk that changes every way you look at it. But not glossy like silk; soft, just drinking in light and giving it back to you melted into color. I had heard of that cape but I had never seen it. I reckon it is the only one in the world to-day. Made of the skins of humming birds—the tiny jeweled ones; thousands and thousands of them; they are no bigger than the tip end of your little finger. *Huitzin* they call them because they are sacred to their god Huitzilopochtli. It means you belong to the family of the king.

But even the *huitzin* cape, even the gold could not make him look like anything but a poor old mummy; not much bigger than a ten-year-old boy, all shriveled down to nothing. Old, old as the hills he looked—the hills out yonder, never caring, as blue for white men as they had ever been for Aztec kings.

I told Gene what little I knew about him, and her eyes got very big and solemn.

"Oh!" she says, whispering. "Is this the vale of Anahuac[70]?"

I was surprised. But it seems she had only read about it in a book—about Moctezuma—Montezuma she calls him—and Guatamotzin and the *noche triste*; the sad night, the Spaniards call it, when Cortez thought the Nahuatlecas was going to run them out in spite of all they could do.

"No," I says. "The valley of Anahuac is near a thousand miles from here. But even a cripple could travel that far in four hundred years."

---

70   Vale of Anahuac. Aztec name for the Valley of Mexico, where Mexico City
       is located.

That is the feeling that you get—like it was old Guatamotzin himself, alive. We kind of talked in whispers, watching him. Then our horses came. The peon that brought them sort of looks at Jimmy like he wanted to say something, but instead of saying it he goes over and kneels down in front of Guatamo. One of the old men translates what he says, and he talks loud because Guatamo is kind of deaf, it seems. And Guatamo moved for the first time since we had been watching him. He raised his head and looked up the hill with those hot, crazy black eyes of his, and made like he was going to stand up. Then he let his head drop and pulled the *huitzin* cape across his face.

"What is it?" says Jimmy, asking me.

"I don't know," I says, lying to him, which I do understand a few words of Nahua from Concha. No, she is not an Aztec; she is a Chichimec[71] but all the main tribes of the Nahuatlecas used to talk the same. That is what Nahuatleca means—talkers of Nahua. But they have mostly forgotten it. That is why this poor old Guatamo had to have an interpreter to talk to his own people.

"I don't know," I says, lying to the kid. "Come on," I says, "let's go!"

But he called the peon and asked him.

"Excuse, Excellency," says the man, "excuse that she spoke of you—but the *mesera*[72]—she who had the misfortune to spill the *mole* on the dress of the señorita—she was telling us how valiantly your grace defied Don Santiago in the dining-room. And Don Santiago came upon us and heard, and he is going to have that rash woman flogged."

"Come on, kid," I says. "There ain't a thing you can do about it."

That was the difference between me and him. I hated it as much as he did, but I knew it was no use interfering and he did not

---

71   Chichimec. A Nahuatl term for a group of indigenous, nomadic peoples who lived north of Mexico City. Similar in meaning to the Roman term "barbarian".

72   Mesera. Waitress.

care whether it was any use or not. He just showed his teeth and whirled his horse and went back up that hill like a bat out of thunder.

Well, sir, I did not know what to do. Like as not that fool kid would go bulging in there and get himself shot, the humor Moreno was in; yet here I had Gene on my hands. I looked at her. I thought she would be kind of scared and sick, but she was plain mad at me.

"Well?" she says. "Aren't you going to help him?"

"Come on!" I says. "We might as well get hung for a sheep as a lamb."

We could not go as fast as Jimmy did, because Gene would have fell off. Come to think of it, a side-saddle is a fool thing anyway. What is the sense of pretending that women have not got legs? What did the good Lord give them legs for if not to use?

I took her by Moreno's house and yelled to her to go in there and stay there. Did you ever see a human whipped? I hope you never do. It is no way to treat a dumb brute, let alone a man or a woman born to walk upright on two legs. They do not do it much these days; only when they want to put the fear of God into them. I reckon Moreno was just crazy mad that day.

I did not see the start of it. I see this crowd of peons in this corral, and this woman with her hands tied up to a post, and Jimmy's horse dancing loose and Jimmy and this sobrestante rolling on the ground. I hit running with my gun in my hand. I was not going to interfere if the fight was fair, but these people do not know how to fight fair. A knife or a gun is all they know.

Wham! goes Jimmy's fist on the *sobrestante's* jaw. The rest of it happened quick as a gun flash; quicker than that, because I did not have time to shoot. Moreno and three or four *sobrestantes* was standing there with guns to keep the peons in order while they got their lesson. But one of the *sobrestantes* whirls to take a crack at Jimmy's head with his gun barrel. A man jumps between us and then there is men all over them.

I kept yanking men by the back of the neck, hauling them off and yelling to Jimmy to come out of that mess. I see a knife sticking out of the back of a khaki coat, and I felt pretty sick because I thought it was him; but it was only the *sobrestante*. Then I hear the kid yelling somewhere.

"Gene! Gene! For God's sake, beat it out of here!"

I might have known that girl would not stay put. She was right there, hopping up and down and shaking Jimmy by the arm.

"Are you hurt? Jimmy! Are you hurt? Are you hurt?"

"Not yet!" says Jimmy, and fairly snatched her feet off the ground.

Moreno went by us; I did not have any idea that fellow could run so fast; but that corral was no place for bosses now. He had nothing to depend on but his *sobrestantes*, and he was losing them rapid. The air was full of machetes, which a machete is something you can lay your hand on any time around an hacienda; it is a tool and a first-class thing to fight with, heavy and sharp and long.

It was no place for me either. My skin is fairly white and they are not taking time to ask me was my grandpa American or Spanish. I know I did not ask who it was when a machete knocked my hat off; I just turned around and shot him and kept going. I remember the whow! whow! of two shots echoing hollow in the *zaguán* of Moreno's house, and Jimmy shoving out a fellow that toppled right on my heels. Then the big wooden doors boomed shut and we were inside, Jimmy and Gene and me and Moreno coughing with powder smoke and asking each other it we were hurt or anything; Elena and the *administrador* and old lady Moreno screeching at us through the bars of the *cancel*.

"Santiago! Santiaguito! *Por dios*[73], what happens?"

---

73   Por dios. Oh, my God!

I Remember the Whow! Whow! of
Two Shots Echoing Hollow in
the Zaguan of Moreno's House,
and Jimmy Shoving Out a Fellow
That Toppled Right on My Heels.

IX

REACH me that bottle over there, will you? I have not talked so much since old Heck was a pup[74]. Usually there is some white man by here every day or so; but it is just my luck that nobody has happened along since this thing broke; and it is pretty lonesome sitting here by myself and thinking. And it is no use talking about it to Concha. All she sees is that Jimmy is gone, and the Morenos are gone, and she can not see anything funny about getting shot behind the ear. She thinks I am drunk because I keep feeling the place and grinning to myself; but I am just thinking how those Indians could not have got in the house if they had not plugged me. I am not kicking. It serves me right for getting old and careless and forgetting that a man can climb a tree.

Drink hearty! Where did I leave off?

---

74   Since old Heck was a pup. Alt: since old Hector was a pup. Hector was the son of King Priam and Queen Hecuba of Troy. Therefore "a long time ago."

Well, there we were. They could not burn the house down because it was adobe[75]. They could have busted the outer *zaguán* doors with a log or something, but the inner door would stop them and we could shoot them through the bars. They could not pull the bars off the windows without getting in front of them. They did try to come at us over the roof—you know how these houses are, a hollow square around the patio—but we heard the ladder going up and me and Jimmy climbed up on the roof and shot the first head that showed, and reached over and threw the ladder down, and got nothing but a few chips of tile in our faces. They are not very good at shooting quick.

But there we were. They could not get in and we could not get out.

"We must get word to the *rurales*[76]," says Moreno, down in the patio watching for somebody to try to bust in a window or a door.

I had to laugh. Up there on the roof I could see the basin spread out empty to the rim of hills; only a few trails of dust where the *vaqueros* had galloped in to help smoke us out, and a few specks of peons hoofing it home; it was as good as a holiday to them.

The nearest *rurales* was at Hosto, fifteen kilometers the other side of there. And their *comandante*[77] was no mind reader. Not so, Bolivia! He is a fat fellow named Nuñez, and all he thinks about is eating and politics, which he had got his job out of the last revolution.

All we could hope for was that word of the trouble would reach Hosto somehow. All we could do was hold out as long as we could. By daylight it was easy; or ought to have been. All we had to do was keep them from climbing on to the roof or sniping us from other roofs; they tried that, but we discouraged them.

---

75   Adobe. A building material usually consisting of bricks made from mud mixed with straw or other organic material.

76   Rurales. The rural defense police, not formalized at the time of this story, a paramilitary force organized to keep peace in the countryside. They were, at times, organized by the revolutionary government.

77   Comandante. Commander.

The other roofs was lower and we could see them easier than they could see us.

But it got awful dull. You can talk about your terrible fixes, but a thing like that is tedious. I reckon it was duller down in the patio. First thing I knew, Gene came scrambling up the vine trellis like a monkey, and I did not have the heart to send her down.

"How come you are not scared?" I says to her.

"I am," says she.

"You sure don't look it," I says, which she has lost her hat, and her short hair is flying up cute, and her gray eyes steady, and her face—I can't explain. Young. That is it. She sits there on the coping[78] and looks a long time off to the hills before she answers.

"I am afraid," she says. "Men—the hates of men—" And she looks at me. "But there is something," she says, "out here. Maybe it is the hills, I'm city bred. I never felt the earth so wide. So big and strong and real. Eternal and infinitely calm. It—it makes panic—an impertinence. It makes a life seem little, and life seem infinitely more. Does that mean anything to you?"

You think it over. She could talk sense as plain as anybody when she tried.

Well, I got careless, sitting there talking, and listening to her and Jimmy. I kept an eye on the roofs, of course; but nothing happened, only the sun went down; and I got careless. I never thought about that big bushy tree sticking up behind the stables, not fifty yards away. And finally a man crawls up into it with a rifle that must have been made in the spring of 'seventy-three, and gets a good rest and takes his time and spatters about half a pound of lead on my thick skull.

It seems I rolled off into the patio and fell on the *administrador* and pretty near broke his back. Gene, she comes flying down to see if I am killed or anything, and Jimmy lies down on the roof and starts shooting up that tree; but a young fellow can not think of two things at once. They got a ladder up and jumped on him

---

78   Coping. The protective cap or cover on a wall.

*"It makes a Life Seem Little, and Life seem Infinitely More.
Does That Mean Anything to You?"*

from behind. They could have knifed him right then; but Indians have got their own way of figuring.

Well, sir, Moreno and the *administrador* gave up. I am not blaming them; they was caught. They would only have got themselves killed fighting, and the women too. They thought I was dead. I thought so, too, till finally my head started to ache something terrible.

The patio was full of Indians. I thought I had gone half blind; I did not realize that I had been unconscious and it was nearly dark. I hear old Guatamo talking, his voice thin and slow, and I see him perched on the edge of the fountain, a few pigeons flapping around and scolding him. King or no king, they did not like him to be sitting there. I did not know enough Nahua to follow what he said; but pretty soon one of the old men starts translating. He was reading Moreno's funeral all the way from Cortez clear down to Porfirio Diaz, blaming him for all that the Spaniards have ever done to them.

I could not see very well for legs and the dusk and my head aching, and I thought I had better keep still till I could figure what to do. This old man is standing right by me. Then I see Moreno all trussed up like a turkey to be roasted, but I could not see Jimmy or Gene anywhere. And I felt pretty sick. I could not help thinking what on earth would I tell Gene's papa when he got back.

"Make ready!" says the old man, solemn.

And they lay Moreno back over a stone bench and tear his shirt open; you know, to cut his heart out. Well, sir, the white man does not live that can stand it. I reached out and grabbed that old hellion's legs from under him. At the same time I hear Jimmy yelling; and I am telling you they could not hold me down. I hit the floor all right, but I came bucking up with Indians all over me. I did not know there was that many Indians in the world.

"How are you getting along?" I yells. "Where's Gene?"

"Right here!" yells Jimmy, bumping up and down like me. But they did not seem to want to knife us. I wondered why.

And then somebody roars, "Hands up!" and there is a commotion right.

The *rurales* had came at last. This fellow Nuñez—this fat *comandante*—his voice is kind of rough and loud, but it was not half rough enough or loud enough to suit me.

I yells, "Hands up! The *rurales!* The *rurales!*" for fear they might not notice it. And I put my hands up, and the Indians that was wrastling with me put theirs up, and pretty soon everybody had them up but Moreno and Jimmy and the ladies, which theirs was tied behind them. Yes, sir, it looked like we was saved. Moreno rolls off the bench and gets up and hops—did you ever see a man try to walk with his feet tied?—and falls down and puts his face on the *comandante's* foot, half crying, he was so grateful.

Nuñez, he just looked down at him and laughed. These *rurales* are a tough bunch and trouble is what they live on. They are good fighters, but it is sure no use expecting them to be sorry for anybody.

"Hoh-hoh-ho!" he roars. "The fine Señor Don Santiago Moreno, he has changed from what his custom is. He does not seem so *orgulloso,* so proud as I have seen him other times. How does it seem to you, boys?" he says, and the *rurales* crowded around and laughed at Moreno squirming on the floor.

But I was busy untying Jimmy and did not pay much attention till I heard Nuñez roar out an order, very military.

"Stand him up! Santiago Moreno," he says, trying to make it sound legal, "in the name of the revolution and the President of the Republic of Mexico I confiscate your estates! Squad Number One! Bring lanterns, torches, anything. Squad Number Two! Take me this *cientifico* out and shoot him!"

Cientificos[79], that is what they call the men that sided with Porfirio Diaz in the old days—mostly rich men and mostly Spanish. Most of them are dead or chased out of the country now—like the

---

79 Científico. Scientists, or scientifics. A group of advisors to president Díaz, proponents of 'scientific politics.'

Terrazas[80] family that used to own pretty near the whole state of Chihuahua; young Terrazas murdered and old Terrazas in Spain and the politicians dividing up his land. But this is an out-of-the-way place. The big politicians never paid much attention to it and the little politicians had never had the nerve to tackle Santiago Moreno.

It hits this Nuñez like an inspiration. Nuñez, he is not a Spaniard and he is not an Indian; he is a revolutionary and a politician, and all he thinks about is eating and playing both ends against the middle. He does not care a thing about Guatamo or the Nahuatlecas, but he is right tickled to realize that they have got Moreno treed for him. It comes to him that he is a made man.

---

80   Terrazas. A large, powerful, influential family based in the Mexican state of Chihuahua. At the time of the Mexican Revolution, they owned upward of 50 haciendas comprising more than seven million acres. They are still powerful in Chihuahua today.

The Proud Old Name

X

IT HITS Moreno different. I felt right sorry for him; I turned around and grabbed Nuñez by the arm.

"Captain," I says, "don't shoot him. Tell him he has got to get out of the country or something. He has had enough trouble without getting shot."

"Squad Number Three!" says Nuñez. "Shoot this gringo too!"

Well, sir, you can not realize that you are going to be shot. Some other fellow, yes; you have seen other fellows dead; but you have always been alive, far as you know, and you have not got much to go by. But I did not make a fuss because I did not want Jimmy and Gene to get messed up in it. I started to walk out; but Jimmy had heard. He could not believe it any more than I did.

"*Señor comandante!*" he says. "Are you crazy? You can't do this!"

"Who says I can't?" says Nuñez, haughty.

"I do!" says Jimmy. What else could he say? "Don Luis is an American!"

"I have shot a hundred Americans," says Nuñez. "Who are you that I should hesitate to shoot you too?"

That is not so, of course. There has not been much more than two hundred Americans killed altogether, and of course he did not kill half of them himself. But there has been plenty of them killed, and durn little ever done about it. Jimmy and me and Gene would only be two or three more.

"Who, me?" says Jimmy. That was not bluff; he was surprised.

"You," says Nuñez. "And why not? Who are you?"

Jimmy, he looks at him a minute. By gum, I wish you could have seen that boy! Smiling and yet not smiling; proud; I can't explain. He was plumb tired of being asked who he was in that tone of voice.

"If you must know," he says, "I am the grandson of old man Brown."

"Brah-oon?" says Nuñez.

"Himself," says Jimmy.

"Exactly!" I answers. "That's who he is. The grandson of old man Brown himself. You mean to tell me you did not know?"

Well, sir, this Nuñez scratched his head. In this country you do not brag about your grandpa unless he is somebody. In Spanish the same as in English, "old man" can mean old man or it can mean the boss. Far as he knew, old man Brown could be the President of the United States; or the Secretary of War; or anybody. And he did not like the quiet way the kid said it, like it was a joke on somebody; Nuñez sure did not want it to be on him.

"Who is the old man Brah-oon?"

"Why," says Jimmy, "my grandfather."

"And Don Santiago is to be the young Señor Brown's father-in-law!" I says. "You had better order him brought back here quick. Do you want the responsibility of shooting the father-in-law of the grandson of old man Brown?"

I wish you had been there. Jimmy, he sees he has got Nuñez going; he just looks him in the eye.

"Quick!" I says. "The young señor does not care about the es-tate; you can have it. If you wish, he will engage that Don Santiago shall leave the country. But his execution is a thing he will not forgive."

"Quick!" says Jimmy.

Nuñez did not know what to do. Exile sounds pretty legal to him, and shooting is a thing he knows all about. But when a man is dead and you wish he was not, there is mighty little you can do about it.

"Can your grace promise that he will go?"

"Bring him here," says Jimmy, "and you will see."

Quiet and confident he says it, looking that fellow in the eye. That is a thing the natives never will understand about a bluff. They know the word from the boys playing poker around here, but they never will know what it means. They think it is just a smart trick; just wind. No, sir, a good bluff is more than just fooling the other fellow about the cards in your hand. It is playing what is in you against what is in him. If Jimmy had not felt the way he did he could not have made it stick. He was the grandson of old man Brown and he was not ashamed of it if he was going to be shot the next minute. And when he saw he had this *comandante* going, he had the nerve to play the hand out without batting an eye.

Drink hearty! The way I look at it, if the stuff is in you, it does not matter where you got it. If not, all the grandpas in the world will not make you different. How do you feel about it?

Huh? Did Moreno promise? You try it some time. Stand up against a wall and look a few rifles in the eye and listen for the word to fire. You will be in the humor to promise anything.

It did not strike me so funny at the time, but riding home that night I had to laugh. The *rurales* camped right there in the patio, which they was not going to let Moreno out of their sight until he was gone; and we went into the *comedor*[81] for a cup of chocolate, because we needed a little something to calm us down. And you ought to have seen them act respectful to that kid.

81　Comedor. Dining room.

"Where do you go?" I says, polite. "To Spain?"

"Say yes, papa!" Elena begs him. "To Spain, papa! To Spain!"

She has been raised to think it is the greatest country in the world. Well, maybe it is—for them. Their kinfolks live there. A good many of their friends have been chased there. And in Spain you can find proud names behind every bush.

"Perhaps," says Moreno, and speaks to Jimmy in a low voice for fear the *rurales* will hear. "Why hast thou not told us, Santiago, that thy grandfather is of importance in the United States?"

Jimmy was looking kind of listless and worn out. "He was not of importance," he says, quiet. "He was a carpenter."

"A—carpenter!" says old lady Moreno. "An architect, perhaps?"

"A carpenter. A worker with his hands. Nor more nor less."

"But thou hast said to this creature Nuñez—

"That he was my grandfather."

"But the manner of thy saying it!" says Elena. "So *orgulloso!* Proud!"

"A joke," says Jimmy. "A jest."

But it was no joke to them. They was plumb cross-eyed for fear the *rurales* would find it out; and how could the grandson of a carpenter protect them?

Jimmy, he sits and looks at them. All of a sudden he kind of kicks me under the table. There is a kind of a look in his face; solemn; I can't explain.

"I am ashamed that I have not told you all," he says. "It is your right to know. My grandfather was a carpenter; my father was a vender[82] of groceries—"

"Groceries!" says Elena, which in this country a grocer is not much.

"—and I myself have served at menial tasks. I have served table, I have been an assistant to a laundry—"

____

82   Vender. Alternate spelling of 'vendor' peculiar to the New Yorker maga-
     zine.

I could have yelled out loud. That durn kid looking down like he was ashamed!

"And my mother," he says, "was a sewing woman. My fortunes go with yours if it is your wish—even to Spain; even to the ends of the—"

"Your fortunes!" says Moreno. "It is perhaps your fortune that you seek! Bloff," he says, which bluff is a word they know— "you *Yanquis*[83] and your bloff! Very nearly it has obtained you fortune and an honorable name!"

"But I confess it now," says Jimmy, humble. "And in Spain there would be few to know, to cast dishonor on your name; only the chance that some man whom I served—it shall be for Elena to say."

"You forget," says Moreno, "that it is I who order in this house!"

He was afraid to trust Elena; but he need not have been. Gene, she could not figure what was happening until then. She looks at me, and I had to look away for fear I would laugh out loud.

"The gate, Jimmy?" she says.

"The air," says Jimmy. "Through with your chocolate? Let's go."

"Amen!" says she. That was the way they talked—no sense to it; but they both seemed to know what they meant.

I kept my face straight until I got outside; but riding home I had to laugh. I laughed so loud that Jimmy and Gene thought I was getting feverish with my head. But not so, Bolivia! I was just thinking. Spaniards and Americans and Indians and Chinamen— every one of them thinks he is better than the others; but the fact is, they are just different. Not only their skins but clear to the backbone. You can change your habits and you can change your name, but you can not change what is in you. What is the use of arguing which is better?

Yes, Jimmy, he was right worried about my head. Next day Ward came back from Siete Minas, and Jimmy asked me, anxious,

---

83 Yanquis. Yankees.

if I could get along all right while he took Ward and Gene to the railroad at Orendain. And then I reckon he decided the railroad was dangerous, too, because a couple of days after that a fellow rode over with a telegram Jimmy had sent from Guadalajara, asking me if my head was all right and saying he was going to run up to the States to buy that machinery I had been trying to get him to buy. But he did not tell me where I could send him a telegram not to go.

That was two–three weeks ago. Then to-day I get another telegram. Wait till I strike a match. I have pretty near wore it out reading it.

"Have been too busy to buy machinery. Married to-day. Will buy machinery on wedding trip. Prepare to extend operations. Ward financing purchase of machinery for one-third interest. Wire your approval care of Hotel Windsor, New York. Look for us home when you see us coming. Grade place for building house. Gene says tell Concha she is a sweet old thing. Love to you both from Mr. and Mrs. James T. Brown."

I do not care what he does with the mine; he can give it to Ward if he wants to; all I want is to hear him joshing people around here. It is pretty lonesome when you get used to having a young fellow around. And if he has simply got to get married it might as well be Gene. She is not much like a woman anyway. There is some sense to a girl like that. She has got backbone. And the biggest thing is something I bet you will think is a little thing. They like the same kind of jokes. They will not get lonesome because they are good friends with each other. Jimmy, he will not have to be telling her she is more beautiful than the stars in the heavens, and she will not have to be telling him he is the bravest, handsomest man in the world. Not so, Bolivia! He will just say to her, "You are the barber-shop kid," and she will say to him, "That is the boy!" And when they have troubles they can josh each other out of them. Yes, and their kids will be husky young gringos and have blue eyes and more freckles than a guinea egg[84], and they

---

84   Guinea egg. Egg of the Guinea hen or Guinea fowl. Noteworthy for its brown speckles.

will call me grandpa or I will tan their bright young hides for them. It is as good a name as any man could want.

That telegram was a day and a half getting here. So to-day I have been trying to make up for lost time, celebrating. But it is kind of lonesome celebrating by yourself; I am sure glad you came along. Drink hearty to the grandson and granddaughter-in-law of old man Brown!

Huh? Oh, Concha feels good about it all right. I showed her the words where Gene said she was a sweet old thing, and she was so tickled she bust right out crying. But it is no use explaining to her about Jimmy's grandpa. She would say that Jimmy is all right even if his grandpa was a carpenter, and I am afraid to try to explain that it is a joke. I am afraid that she might think it is on her.

THE END

Not So, Bolivia

Not So, Bolivia

FOREWORD

How happy I was to discover this little-known sequel to The Proud Old Name! It was originally published in the Saturday Evening Post of April 24, 1926.

Uncle Lew is back and up to his old shenanigans, along with Jimmy, Gene, and a newcomer!

I hope you will enjoy seeing Uncle Lew in action again as much as I have.

Not So, Bolivia and its original illustrations by D. H. W. Koerner are all now in the public domain.

Jimmy Saw This Long Painted Canoe Go Slipping Along Down in That Canyon, Old Guatamo Huddled in His Huitzin Cape

I

HELLO, Jimmy. What did you think when I pretended like I did not know you? I did not want them to find out you was my partner. Did you notice that thin fellow with the black-rimmed specs? Excuse me for laughing, Jimmy. They brought him in to see if I was lying. They think I am too drunk to see straight, but not so, Bolivia! I am an old fool and I talk too much with my mouth, but I got out of it all right. If they get to thinking about it and come fooling around us out home, you can just laugh and say I am an old fellow that is always talking through my hat, and I will prove it to them. I will just feed them the wildest yarn I can make up, and then get mad and run them all off because they think I am a liar.

They will not get anything out of Concha, that is a sure thing. She will just look at them like she does not understand their brand of Spanish, and does not know anything worth saying anyway. You know how Indians are.

It was all right till they run in this doctor on me. I cannot figure him, Jimmy. He does not act like a doctor; more like a school-teacher or something; and the other two are both tenderfeet[85], but he knows what he is talking about. He knows about the Aztecs and the Nahua[86] empire. He cannot talk Spanish very good, but he could read the Aztec writing on that piece of gold, or claimed to; and he pretty near went crazy when I told him I had seen Guatamo's cave.

Hold your horses, Jimmy. I am not claiming I was not a fool. But after you and Gene and the baby got on the train, I felt kind of lost and low in my mind, because I will miss the little devil. Did he do anything cute on the train? Did Gene make her connection at Irapuato[87] all right? I bet A. T. will sure be proud to see his grandson. I hope he teaches him to say grandpa, so maybe he will call me grandpa too.

I did not know what to do with myself. I do not hardly know a soul in Guadalajara. I do not like cities, Jimmy. They make me lonesome for the hills. Strangers whizzing around you till you cannot rest—you feel like it does not matter what you say, because they do not know you and you will never see them again. I will be glad to get back home where we do not have to fool with trains, but just get on our horse and go.

I stayed in bed till pretty near eight o'clock. I walked around all morning, and got my shoes shined two-three times so I could talk to the bootblacks. I dropped around to old Juan Murphy's store to get him to have a drink with me, but he was busy with some customers. So I walked around the plaza and had my shoes shined again, but it was lonesome sitting there just looking at the palace and the cathedral and a thousand people going by, and nobody to talk to after the bootblack found another customer.

So I thought I would step up here to the American Club, because I might as well get some good out of the money you made me spend to join it. But there was not a soul I knew. I had to show

---

85 Tenderfoot. Newbies, inexperienced persons, especially those new to a rough area or region.

86 Nahua. Indigenous people of Mexico and Central America. Thought to be the ancestors of the Aztecs and Toltecs.

87 Irapuato. A city in central Mexico approximately 150 (245 km) miles east of Guadalajara.

my card, because they did not think I was a member. There was a poker game going on, but they were all city men and looked like they was afraid I would put my foot on their chair. I would have walked out, but they would have thought I was embarrassed.

So I sat down at a table by myself and had a drink or two, but it did not do me any good. It was sure lonesome, Jimmy. Along about sundown the game began to peter out because some of them had to go home to supper, but they did not ask me to take a hand. I reckon they thought I did not have money enough. I could not help thinking how they would look if I told them about that cave full of gold idols and silver herons and curiosities like that.

Finally there was only two of them left, and the bartender. This big fellow says he will buy one more drink, and he took to showing his friend something out of his pocket, which he said he was going to ask this Doctor Somebody about it. He said it was a piece of Aztec money, but of course you know—

Not So, Bolivia

II

EXCUSE me, sir. I could not help hearing what you said. That is not money. The Aztecs did not—Huh? Let me see it and maybe I can tell you. Yes, it looks like the real thing all right. This ring is not welded on like white men do it; it is all hammered out of one piece. But it is not money. More likely it is a thing they wore on their foreheads, on a wooden band around their hair, and showed whether they was nobles or priests or warriors or just laboring men. Huh? Because they did not have money. They used turkey quills full of gold dust, with cacao beans for small change.

No, I reckon they did not have as much gold as people say. Most of their big statues are just gold plated. No, not like we do; they made a mold out of clay and charcoal, and covered the inside with gold dust and poured in melted copper or a mixture of gold and copper, and the gold dust melted and made it look like solid gold. Huh? Because I have seen them. Some of them are hollow and you can see the copper inside.

But the statue of Huitzilopochtli[88] is pure gold. That is their war god; he is the one Guatamo prays to all the time, asking Huit-

---

88 Huitzilopochtli. Aztec god of the sun, war, and human sacrifice.

zil' to tell him when it is time to kill all the white men and bring back the day of Nahuatl glory.

Guatamo? Oh, he is a crazy old Indian out in my district that claims to be their king. He claims to be descended from Guatemotzin—the *tzin* Guatamo; maybe you call him Guatemoc[89]—the prince that killed his uncle Moctezuma[90] to save him from the Spaniards. The walls of his cave are covered with writing like on this gold piece, which he claims it is the history of what has happened since the Spaniards—Sir?

No, sir, I did not say he had it; I said he prayed to it.

Excuse me, gentlemen, for butting in. I—Sir? Well, you can see them for yourself in the museum at Mexico City. Yes, there may be some of them still scattered around the hills. No, sir. I—I could not say exactly. I am just telling you what the Indians claim. I—

Well, sir, I do not mind. Much obliged; I take it kind of you. Drink hearty, gentlemen!

No, I have not got anything to do. I am just waiting for my partner, which he is shipping his wife and baby to the States and has gone with them as far as Irapuato. I admit I was right lonesome. You ought to see that baby, gentlemen. He is sure a buster[91]. He is not much bigger than a minute, but he will grab anything you give him like a bull pup, and you can hoist him right out of his cradle and he will just hang on and grin. A regular gringo[92], he is. His eyes are blue and his hair is yellow, what there is of it; he takes that after Jimmy; his mamma's hair is nearly black.

But she is pure American. Gene Ward, her name was; Eugenia Ward, but everybody calls her Gene because her hair is cut short like a boy and she wears pants riding horseback. It made quite a scandal when she first came down from the States, but they have

---

89   Guatemoc. Cuauhtemōc, the last Aztec Emperor, 1520-1521.

90   Moctezuma. Moctezuma II, penultimate emperor of the Aztec Empire, 1502-1520.

91   Buster. A particularly sturdy or robust child.

92   Gringo. A foreigner, especially a North American.

got used to her and now they think she is just what the doctor ordered.

She is the daughter of old A. T. Ward. Know him? Well, he is one of the vice presidents of Siete Minas[93], out in my district, and owns stock in our mine too. I understand he is quite a fellow in New York. Quite a rich man, I reckon; but Jimmy is not his son-in-law. Not so, Bolivia! It is the other way about. People just put up with A. T., out our way, because of Jimmy marrying his daughter, which A. T. will be a tenderfoot as long as he lives. He never comes down here if he can help it. He thinks Gene is crazy to want to live out in the hills.

Not that he says much. It would not do him any good. Gene, she knows her own mind—yes, and yours too, if you start arguing with her. I do not know how she does it, but she makes you feel like you have been agreeing with her all the time. She can just—Huh?

Sure the Aztecs knew how to alloy gold. They knew some things no white man knows to-day. Like making copper hard as steel. Like their vegetable dyes, still bright after five hundred years. Like the way they lacquered wooden boxes—nobody knows how to do that now but one old man down in Morelos, and his son, and you could kill them and they would not tell you. It is a great pity when you come to think of it. They would have showed us what they knew, but the Spaniards called them savages and burned their books, and burned a good many of the Indians too; and now they are everlastingly afraid.

Yes, sure they had books. Yes, on paper. They made it out of maguey[94] pulp. Huh? You must be newcomers in this country. What we call century plant. Have you ever tasted pulque[95] or

---

93   Siete Minas. (Seven Mines). Possibly based on nearby Cinco Minas (Five Mines).

94   Maguey. Any of several species of Agave.

95   Pulque. A mild alcoholic beverage made from the sap of the maguey plant.

mescal[96]? No, it is not much of a drink for a white man; but that is what they make out of maguey. Once it was more useful to them than even cotton—they made a hundred things out of it; but now they only use it for cheap liquor. That is what white men have done for them.

Sir? Well, maybe I am kind of partial to the Indians. I married one of them.

Oh, that is all right, sir. I am not ashamed of it. I am not saying it is at good thing for a white man or an Indian either; but a young fellow gets lonesome out in the hills, and does not see things like he will when he gets older. I am not kicking. I am just as much of a foreigner to her as she is to me, and she puts up with me. I do not make fun of what she believes, and she found out thirty years ago it was no use trying to understand a white man's notions.

Like the time she found out Gene's baby was coming. Concha, she thinks Gene is the finest girl God ever made, and she was not willing to risk it with the American doctor from Siete Mines and the Spanish priest from Hosto. Concha is a Christian all right, but she was not taking any chances. She had to go and pray to Centeotl[97], and that is how I happened to get to see this—Huh?

Oh, Centeotl means the earth gods. It was the name of a man god and a woman god too; the woman Centeotl had charge of the fruit crops and the harvests and the babies that were born; she was the one the women prayed to when a baby was coming. And if a woman died, Centeotl took her to heaven with the warriors that were killed in fighting.

And when you come to think of it, that is a fine thing to believe. Even if we know it is not so. A woman is just as scared of dying as a man, and in this world there are some risks you cannot get away from; and it helps, to think we are going to get rewarded for being brave. And how do we know it is not so? I do not know

---

96   Mescal. A strong distilled alcoholic beverage made from the maguey plant.

97   Centeotl. The god of maize and subsistence; corresponds to Chicomecoatl, the goddess of agriculture.

about you, but I have tried being scared and I have tried standing up to it like a man; and I know there is something, somehow, that makes me feel better, even if I get hurt worse.

Gene, she was not scared. Not so, Bolivia! That kid does not think much about herself; she is too busy just—just being alive; I can't explain. She likes the hills, though she was raised in cities and just happened to come down here with her papa and meet Jimmy. She is not very big—she looks more like a little boy in her riding clothes, but there is sure something about her. The way her short hair bushes up around her face, careless and eager some-how. The way she moves, like she was happy to be doing it. The way her gray eyes look at you, not laughing always, but always honest and clear and brave. I can't explain.

The only time I ever saw her lose her nerve was once when Jim-my rode out into the hills and was missing for four days, and then come staggering in on foot, his right arm broken and an arrow hole through his left shoulder, and says he has found the cave where old Guatamo lives.

No, no, I will buy this one. H-s-st! See what the gentlemen will have.

Not So, Bolivia

III

THAT is bad country to get lost in, gentlemen. It is not only hills; it is cut up with canyons and *barrancas*[98] a mile deep, all running into each other every which way, and if you get lost in one of them you never know where you are going to get out. And some of them have got water in them, but not many. If you get hurt and cannot travel, the chances are nobody will ever know what became of you but the buzzards.

Yes, Gene was sure scared that time. We did not even know which way he started; you cannot pay attention every time your partner gets on his horse, especially a human steam engine like Jimmy, that is always doing something that pops into his head. The first night she said he was all right, just staying somewhere, which he never did without telling her. But she took to walking the floor, and every now and then she would stop and look around her like she was lost herself. Like she had never seen that house before. This was when they was first married, and their house was nice and new, all furnished with a piano and things

---

98   Barrancas. A barranca is a steep canyon or ravine.

packed in by mule; but she would sure not feel at home if he was gone.

So I shut down the mine and told the men to scatter, hunting him. I stayed with Gene to keep her pacified, but the second night I could not stand it. So l fixed up a heavy block shot[99] and told her to fire the fuse if he showed up. Two days and nights I went hollering up and down *barrancas* like a crazy man; and then just at daylight I saw buzzards flocking over the river about five miles up a canyon from where I was, and they was picking the fresh bones of a shod horse. The way the bones was busted showed he had come bumping down that cliff two thousand feet.

And it was Jimmy's horse; I knew the way our blacksmith shod him; and finally I found his saddle, what was left of it, because that horse had hit the rocks a dozen times before the cinch had broke. Well, sir, I was just crazy. I could see places where he might have lodged, but could not climb to them. I yelled myself black in the face, and I would hold my breath and listen, and everything was still as death for about a minute; and then my own voice would come bellowing back like fifty giants laughing. All of a sudden I saw a naked hill Indian watching me, but when I yelled at him he just went out like smoke. I could not even find the place he had been standing.

You get queer notions, out there by yourself that way.

So I rode back a few miles to where I could climb out, and up on the mesa I picked up Jimmy's trail. He had been riding along the edge of the *barranca*. There was an Indian pueblo[100] a ways back, but I could not get anything out of them. They just looked at me; you know how these hill Indians do. A good many of them do not know Spanish, and if they are scared you cannot be sure any of them do. And they was scared, all right. A dozen of them trailed me to the place the horse had fell, watching me like a hawk, with bows and arrows.

---

99   Block shot. A mining technique involving explosives.
100   Pueblo. A village.

Yes, some of the hill tribes use them still. Too poor or too igno-rant to buy guns. Think of it, gentlemen; a million dollars' worth of gold idols and featherwork and jeweled altars right there un-der their feet, and them looking and living like the tail end of hard times!

Sir? No, sir, I did not find the cave. I am just telling you about my partner. Any other white man would have got himself killed for finding out what he did, but not Jimmy. Not so, Bolivia! But do not let me keep you from your supper, gentlemen. I am afraid I get pretty talkative when l have a drink or two.

No, much obliged. I have not finished this one.

Sir? Yes, I thought sure the boy was gone. You could see where his horse had been standing, fidgeting like horses do, and where he made a jump and slipped and fell. And I felt sure those Indi-ans knew what made him jump. And I felt ugly, I am telling you. It did not seem like it was any use if a fine, upstanding, likable young fellow could get killed, which he had everything to live for, and I am just a useless old hard-shell[101] that has done every-thing wrong but get him for a partner. I felt like killing me a few Indians and getting them to kill me, because I could not stand to look Gene in the eye and tell her.

You could see bushes broke where he had fell. You could see ledges where he might have lodged, but you could not climb down to them; and likely he would never live to hit them. Just down and down in jumps of fifty to five hundred feet, the river looking like a little silver branch and the green bushes turning blue, and a few black dots moving. Those were the buzzards that had looked so high down there.

Calling and calling to him, and never a whisper but your own voice ha-ha-ing up again. Like the hills mocking you. Empty they look, but they have seen men crawling here like ants—fighting like ants; they have seen armies of two hundred thousand men, that could kill each other with arrows and spears and flint-studded war clubs just as well as we can with guns. God knows how many

---

101 Hard-shell. A hardback; a tough person that is hard to beat or wont go
     down easily.

thousand years. We think Aztecs are old, but the Chichimecs[102] was here, already civilized, when Aztecs was just savages from somewhere north, hiring themselves out for fighting men. The Toltecs was already dying out. The Mayas had gone south so long ago that nobody knows when they was here, but they have yarns to show they came this way—about the Long Night, and the sun that came up like the moon and circled low on the horizon, and water that froze to let them walk across.

Always and always from the north. From Tlapallan[103]; but nobody knows just where Tlapallan was. All they remember is the Seven Caves they lived in, and Big Water, and the herons. That is what Aztec means—Heron People. That is why they have these gold and silver herons. That is where Guatemotzin[104] was making for, four hundred years ago, after the Spaniards tricked them and wiped out their armies. He was trying to lead his people back to Tlapallan, but he got so far and died.

Races and kings and centuries crawling by. Praying and fighting; loving, hoping, trying—dying and vanishing. What for?

Sometimes you feel like these blue hills could tell you. You think of it at night, out there, seeing them stand so big and calm against the stars. You think God must have put them there to make a man think big. You think it must mean something when a man can feel so much—so many things besides just hungry or afraid.

But sometimes, gentlemen, they are too big for you. Like nightmares. Monstrous and deaf and blind and everlasting; like a man does not amount to anything—standing there on the edge of a *barranca* like a flea on the edge of hell, and nothing but your own voice cursing back at you.

And then I heard that block shot go. Not loud; I was full twenty miles away; but no gun makes a noise like that. You hear it through the ground. Bung! And then a long slow booming afterward. Well, sir, I gave those Indians a lesson in disappearing. I

---

102 Chichimec. A Nahuatl term for a group of indigenous, nomadic peoples who lived north of Mexico City. Similar in meaning to the Roman term "barbarian".

103 Tlapallan. An unidentified location in the Aztec origin mythology.

104 Guatemotzin. Another name for Cuauhtemōc.

bet I burned a streak across that mesa. I bet I jumped that horse across *barrancas* a mile wide.

And there was that durn Jimmy safe in bed and raving with high fever, which he had no business traveling with an arm broke and an arrow through his shoulder.

Out of his head and cooing like a calf.

"Naya" he says. "Naya! Where art thou, sweetheart? Come!"

IV

THERE is no woman at our place named Naya. And once in a while he muttered something about Ixtaccicoyotl … Huh? Why, there is nothing tricky about it. Ish-toc-cee, white; co-yotl, fox—White Fox. It is a man's name. Concha—she is my wife—she did not know anything about this Naya woman, but when he said White Fox she pretty near turned white herself. She tried to make him hush, and said a prayer to Huitzilopochtli, and crossed herself, which Concha gets her gods mixed up sometimes.

"Who is White Fox?" I asked her.

But she just give me one look and threw her hands up like we are all ruined, and went off praying to Huitzil'. There are some things they will not tell you, even if you are married.

Neither would Jimmy. He was all right next day, but pretty sick, and did not know he had been talking; and he had a fish story all made up to tell us. He said he had been hunting one of our mules that had broke out and strayed, and had picked up her trail and was following it when he run into these Indians.

"I saw your trail all right," I says, "but no mule tracks."

"Not up on the mesa," says Jimmy. "I lost her trail in the canyon and climbed up there to see if I could catch sight of her. And the first thing I knew, these arrows started whizzing."

And he tried to look innocent and surprised. But he is not a good liar. Not so, Bolivia! There is not a dishonest bone in that boy's body; it does not come natural; he is too durn careful about it.

"I didn't know those Indians were hostile," says he.

"They did not shoot at me," says I.

"I must have startled them," says Jimmy.

"Just riding along?" says I.

"Yeah," says Jimmy.

"Your hoof prints showed," I says, "your horse was standing quite a while in that one place."

"I stopped to admire the scenery," says Jimmy.

"How did you startle them," I says, "standing still?"

He had to grin. But you cannot faze that boy.

"Maybe they thought I was making faces at them," says he.

But I was mad at him. I always felt like he was square as the day is long; I could not stand to think of him running around and fooling with other women and calling them sweetheart, and a girl like Gene walking the floor and twisting her hands and feeling like she would die if anything happened to him. She was still looking kind of pale and young.

"All right," I says, speaking short. "What next?"

"Some of the arrows must have hit the horse," says he, "because he went over the bluff. I managed to catch a bush with one hand, but the arrow in my shoulder made me sick; I couldn't hang on. I must have hit a ledge. The next I knew I was in—in an Indian shack in the pueblo."

"How come?" I says. "If they are hostile like you say, how come they did not finish killing you off?"

"When they got a good look at me," says Jimmy, "they saw I was too beautiful to die."

He is a scamp, that boy. But I was mad at him, account of Gene. I would not let him make me laugh.

"As beautiful," I says, "as Naya?"

That jarred him; it had him wondering how I knew. Gene, she tried to hush me up; she did not want him to tell anything he did not want to; but I was mad. Many a young fellow has made a mess of things that way. Some of these Indians are real pretty when they are young.

"You heard me," I says, speaking sour. "Who is Naya?"

"Oh," says Jimmy, "she's a—an old woman that nursed me."

"That was real nice of her," I says, sarcastic. "Since when have you been calling old women sweetheart?"

"I mean," says Jimmy, "she is a little girl."

But he had to grin. I can't explain; you may know the boy is lying, but you cannot help feeling like he is all right.

"Uncle Lew," he says—he calls me uncle all the time, though I am no kin to him, only an old fellow that never had a son of my own—"Uncle Lew," he says, "that's my story and I've got to stick to it. Please don't ask me any questions, because I can't answer you. And I can't even tell you why."

"That is the boy!" says Gene. "Spoken like a true Trevelyan[105]!"—whatever a Trevelyan is. And she sits by him and holds his hand and tries to laugh to me, but tears come in her eyes, she was so glad to have him alive and in his right mind. "Roll your hoop[106]," she says, "Uncle District Attorney Lew! Banana oil[107] is out."

That is the way those kids talk half the time. Roll your hoop means lay off of him and pull your freight[108]. That is the boy

---

105 Trevelyan. A line of British civil servants. This exact reference is obscure. Possilby the 1st Baronet Trevelyan, who was known for sticking blindly to his own sense of ethics.

106 Roll your hoop. Leave, get along, move out.

107 Banana oil. Nonsense, flattery.

108 Pull your freight. Leave.

means he is all right. Banana oil means he need not make up any fish stories, because we know he has got a good reason if he does not tell. You can understand them fine when you are used to it. And Jimmy's voice gets husky and says he has heard of wives, but she is sure the berries[109]; which means she is the one that hung up the stars and the moon[110].

What could I do? I says, "Well, why didn't you say so in the first place?" and snorted and walked out.

But something had sure happened to that boy. His arm got well and his shoulder got well, and he went through the motion of working the same as ever, but his mind was sure not on it. Sometimes he could be looking right at you and never hear a word you said. He would give orders and forget that he had give them; and, gentlemen, you cannot run a mine that way; it is a mercy he did not get somebody killed. It had me worried, I am telling you. I did not like the look that came into his face sometimes—his eyes deep-set and hot somehow, and some- thing pinched and wicked around the mouth. It did not seem like Jimmy.

One month we made the biggest clean-up we had ever made, but he did not let out a whoop the way I thought he would. He just says, "That's good. That's fine," more absent-minded; like it was all right, far as it went, but not much berries when you came to think of it.

Evenings, he would sit and stare off at the hills. Even with Gene; and, gentlemen, that does not go. You may trust your husband, but if you are human, a thing like that will sure get on your nerves; especially if there is a woman in it. And Gene's nerves was not any too good about this time. I thought she was just worried about Jimmy; but it seems there was a reason. You know how women are.

Never, gentlemen, tell a married man anything—not if his wife loves him. I am not saying she nagged him; Gene is not that kind.

---

109 The berries. Something wonderful or very good.
110 The one that hung up the stars and the moon. The most wonderful and important person ever.

More likely she was just so easy to talk to that he did not realize that he was breaking his word, which he had swore not to tell. I know that kid; he will keep his word or break a leg. But a man cannot help being anxious about his wife when she had got trouble enough without being worried about him, and wanting to pacify her. It seems he told her—more like it was a joke, so she would not be scared.

And she was not. That is the trouble with telling half the truth. Somebody may believe you, and what you did not tell will blow up in your face.

That durn kid had been spying on Guatamo. That is this old Aztec I was telling you about; the one that claims to be their king. He claims to be descended from Guatemotzin. The Spaniards say Guatemotzin was killed by Cortez after Moctezuma died, but the Indians claim he got away and headed north into the hills, trying to find the way back to the lost country where all the Nahua peoples came from; but he only got about a thousand miles and settled in that cave and died.

I am not saying it is so; I am just telling you. They claim he was the one that brought all these gold idols and altars from Tenochtitlan[111]—the Town of Tenoch—in the valley of Anahuac[112]; what we call Mexico City now.

Jimmy, he was not thinking of the gold; not then. He was just out there hunting that Betsy mule like he said, when all of a sudden he saw this long painted canoe go slipping along down in that canyon, these naked hill Indians paddling, and old Guatamo huddled in his *huitzin*[113] cape. He knew who it was, all right; he could see the sun on his gold headband, though he was two thousand—Huh? No, not a crown. It is a thing they wore to hold their hair, but his is gold instead of wood. Yes, he wears plenty of gold; his poor old bones are fairly loaded with it; even his sandals are gold, though it does not do him much good because he cannot

---

111 Tenochtitlan. The historic center of Mexico City.
112 Valley of Anahuac. Old name for the Valley of Mexico, in which Mexico City is located.
113 Huitzin. Nahuatl word for 'hummingbird.'

walk much. Some fellows caught him once and burned his feet up trying to make him tell where the gold idols was hid out.

Huh? No, I reckon not. They never came back alive. Likely their hearts was burned on the very altars they was looking for. That is the old Aztec way of worshiping Huitzil'—cutting a man's heart out alive; but nowadays they do not have the prisoners to practice on.

Guatamo is a bad man to go fooling with. Himself, he could not hurt a fly, but there are a million Indians that will sure get you if you lay a finger on him. And Jimmy knew it, too; but you know how young fellows are. He did not stop to think. All of a sudden it came to him that maybe he could find out where Guatamo lived, which is a thing no white man ever knew. So he kept out of sight and trailed along, and all of a sudden the canoe turned square at the cliff and went into it and out of sight. And he was sitting up there on his horse, noticing the landmarks so he could find the hole, when arrows started flying.

The next he knew was in Guatamo's cave. They took him there to see if the old hellion[114] wanted to cut his heart out.

Jimmy, he did not tell Gene that. Gene, she had seen Guatamo once; fact is he had more or less to do with her and Jimmy getting married. When Gene first come down here, she just happened to be staying at our house because it was not safe for her to ride on up to Siete Mines with her papa, and me and Jimmy took her over to see Moreno's hacienda[115]. Moreno is one of the richest men in my district, mostly Spanish and very proud, which his daughter was the girl Jimmy was engaged to at the time.

And old Guatamo, he come down out of the hills to have a talk with Moreno about mistreating Indians. These peons have been kicked around by rich men for four hundred years, but now they are sort of getting their hopes up again since the revolutions have

---

114 Hellion. A rowdy, mischievous person.

115 Hacienda. A plantation or estate, Mexican style. Before the Mexican Revolution of 1910–1920, haciendas were owned by the very wealthy and worked by peons who were, for practical purposes, bound to the land like serfs in the feudal system.

A Big Torch Burning Like a Candle by the Dead, and the Princess Naya Kneeling by Him, Fanning, and Staring at Him With Her Big Black Eyes

run so many Spaniards out of the country. I do not know what Guatamo thought he could do about Moreno shooting and whipping his own servants; you cannot get them to stand up to their own master in cold blood. But he come down the river below the hacienda, and they all quit work and flocked down there to get his blessing.

It is right funny, gentlemen. There was this queer old king of slaves down by the river, thinking of things four hundred years ago. There was the Morenos, rich and polite, thinking Gene was plumb scandalous because she had short hair and a short dress and a hat on. There was Jimmy, engaged to Elena and in love with Gene, being Spanish one minute and American the next, and putting his foot in his mouth every time he opened it. And there was me, doing my durnedest to keep the mess from blowing up completely; which it did. Moreno got mad at Jimmy, account of Gene, but Jimmy made him back down and apologize, and Moreno had to take his spite out on somebody. So him and his overseers waded into Guatamo's camp meeting and knocked those peons key west and crooked[116], just to show them who was boss around there.

He did not touch Guatamo; he knew better; but he herded them into a corral like cattle, and he had one of them tied up and whipped, the overseers holding them in line with guns to get their lesson. And Guatamo knew it and could not do a thing.

But Jimmy would not stand for it. Not so, Bolivia! He made one dive at the overseer with the whip and whaled the daylights out of him. So the other overseers turned their back to take a crack at Jimmy, and the Indians jumped on them and there was one great-granddaddy of a scrap. You ought to been there, gentlemen. They come pretty near carving us all before the rurales[117] came.

---

116 Key west and crooked. From 'hell west and crooked,' all over the place; every which way.

117 Rurales. The rural defense police, not formalized at the time of this story; a paramilitary force organized to keep peace in the countryside. They were, at times, organized by the revolutionary government.

Moreno, he had to leave the country for a while. You cannot blame him much for being sore at Jimmy; but he got over it, because Elena married a duke or something while they was hiding out in Spain. The duke is living on Moreno now.

Guatamo, he just faded back into the hills. He is an easy fellow to forget. Years can go by and you will never hear a whisper of him. Even when you are looking at him, he does not seem exactly real—shriveled and wrinkled till he does not look human, wrapped in his *huitzin* cape, more like an old, old crippled bird. You see his eyes, shiny and black and still, and do not realize that he is seeing you. But he can see all right; and he does not forget. A year or two is nothing to a man that can remember back four hundred years.

So when they brought the kid to him in the cave, he saw it was the same freckled young Yankee that kept an Indian from being flogged once. So he did not cut his heart out. He had him put to bed and sent his own great-great-grandniece or something in to fan him.

That was what Jimmy saw when he came to. He says if he had been a turkey he would have thought he was in paradise; but I do not know what turkeys have got to do with gold and beautiful girls. I reckon he was just joshing. That boy would joke to be hung.

But you cannot blame him for feeling queer. Lying on this soft mat with a soft catskin for a cover, a feather canopy over him, soft rich colors running up to this gold plate with jewels shining in the middle; gold on the walls, and feather draperies, and silver herons, and no roof that he could see; a big torch burning like a candle by the dead, and the Princess Naya kneeling by him, fanning, and staring at him with her big black eyes. No wonder mining did not seem much berries to him any more!

Huh? Much obliged; the same. I take it kind of you.

V

NO WONDER he could not take much interest in our monthly clean-up; he had seen more gold than we could dig out of the ground in twenty years. Big chairs of it, carved plates of it, statues of it—gold! Soft, shining, heavy yellow gold, already mined and worked, and nothing to do but kill a few men and cart it off. Oh, I am not blaming him! Old as I am and little good as it would do me, I have waked up in a cold sweat from thinking of that one big statue of Huitzil'. Solid, it must be, and pure gold, or pretty near. I got a chance to heft it once when old Guatamo was not looking, and I could not even joggle it, though I am stouter than you think. And you can see how soft it is by the way it is dented where it fell once on the rocks—while they was bringing it from Anahuac, I reckon, four hundred years ago. I bet some peons got their hearts cut out for that.

Sir?

Yes, I have been there. But that was afterward, like I was telling you; when Concha went to pray about Gene's baby. But do not let me keep you, gentlemen. I am just killing time.

No, much obliged. I do not like my drinks to come so fast. When I was a young fellow I did not know any better, but now I know a man can use only so much of anything—liquor, or victuals, or comfort, or even gold. Gold! There is no liquor that can make a man so drunk or keep him drunk so long. Gold fever—I have had it, gentlemen. I hate to think how many years I wasted on the trail and how I acted when I made my strike at last. But it burns out like any other fever. There comes a day when you wake up with a dry heart, like the dry mouth of a morning after, and wonder what you thought your gold would buy.

Jimmy was not my partner then. I had nobody to be glad for but just Concha, and she never cared. Indians are queer that way. Year after year she trailed with me—the hills did not seem lonesome to her; she was satisfied. She starved with me because I was her man. But she is not a lady, gentlemen; not the way we mean. She did not know how to stop work and live on money. That is why a few thousand dollars went sour on me, the way a million would on you.

Sir? Well, I have never had a million either, but I know it would not do me any good. I would rather just have something to be working at, and a young fellow to be always joshing about it, and a girl like Gene to keep him satisfied, and a husky little gringo growing up to call me grandpa or I will know the reason why. A baby has got a right to have two grandpas, and Jimmy's papa died.

Guatamo can keep his gold, for all of me. Oh, I am not blaming Jimmy! He is young and full of life, and things get hold of him. He could not help figuring how it could be done. He knew it was no use to tackle that cave with guns; you would get stuck full of arrows before you saw a thing to shoot at. No use to try to sneak inside in a canoe; he had seen the mantrap in that tunnel. But we have learned ways of killing people that they never heard of.

There is a cold wind sucking into the tunnel day and night. He figured how you could throw down bombs of gas, like in the German war, and then sit back and smoke your pipe until they was all dead.

He did not tell Gene that. Not so, Bolivia! It seems he made more of a joke of it with her. Those kids can have fun out of anything. They called it Allie Barber[118] and his Forty Thieves, though I never heard of Guatamo or his Indians stealing anything; it is from a yarn about a man that had a cave full of gold. And this girl Naya, they called her Fat Emma[119], though she is not fat or nothing like it. She is a slim girl and durn beautiful.

He did not tell me anything. But I could see him thinking, and once or twice I tried to talk to him.

"Son," I says, "something is eating you, and has been ever since you had that trouble with the Indians. Sometimes it helps to get a thing off your chest. Don't you want to come clean with me?"

"No," says Jimmy—short like that.

"Then I'll tell you," says I. "I can see through a grindstone all right if it has got a hole in it. While you was out of your head you said something about Ixtaccicoyotl—about White Fox," I says, "and Concha was scared green. She will not tell me, and there is only one thing she is scared to talk about, and that is anything that has got anything to do with Guatamo. You have found out something."

"Interesting," says Jimmy, "if true."

"Yeah." I says, and watched his eyes to see if they would flicker. "Is it a woman, Jimmy? Or gold?"

They did not flicker. They did worse. They got kind of hard and blank. I can't explain. Looking straight at me, but not letting me see into them; like something pulled over them. I can't explain.

"Pay your money," says he, short and ugly, "and take your choice[120]."

Yes, and he even figured how he could get the gold out of the country. You could not ship gold idols and old Aztec things; the Government would take them away from you. But we have got

---

118 Allie Barber. Ali Baba, an Arabian folk tale in which an honest-but-poor woodcutter discovers the secret hideout of a den of thieves.

119 Fat Emma. "Fatima"

120 Take your choice. "You pays your money and you takes your choice." It's up to you—pick one.

our own smelter and ship bullion[121] every month. That was how far he had already gone in thinking—melting down statues that people have worshiped for a thousand years, to say nothing of killing men.

But I believe he would have took it out in thinking. A nice young fellow cannot start robbing and murdering in cold blood. I do not think he would ever have gone near that cave again if it had not been for Concha.

He seemed to be forgetting it; or maybe the idea of his son coming along kind of put it out of his mind. He was right worried about Gene. Her health was fine, but—Are you married, gentlemen? Then you will know Gene was not going crazy; but Jimmy did not; this is their first. She started taking queer manias. One while she took to fretting about dust settling on top of the door and window frames where she could not see it, though their house had not been built more than a year, and the air is clean out there. She could not rest until the women climbed up there and scrubbed them.

But shucks! I remember our storekeeper's wife—once she took to hankering for ice cream, which she had never tasted any but about three times in her life, and she pretty near pestered Gonzalo into sending all the way to Orendain for some. He did not do it; they do not humor women much; they figure having babies is just their regular—Huh?

I was just telling you. One day Jimmy comes storming over to my house and yells at me, "Where's Concha?"

This was at noon, and I had not more than got into the house, but I could hear the women getting dinner; I did not think a thing. "Around the house somewhere," I says. "But, son, I am not deaf."

A deaf man could have heard him all right. He went storming through the house and out the back and around to the front again, yelling and calling them. "Gene! Gene! Concha!" But Gene and Concha did not answer. He went tearing down to the river

---

121 Bullion. Gold or silver smelted into bars or ingots, not yet coined.

and back again; and men going by from the mine stopped with their mouth open to see what was the matter.

You could hear him all over the place, but nothing answered. Only faint echoes rolling down out of the hills behind the house, like something laughing, far away and still. I had to grab hold of him to make him tell me.

"The women say they left right after breakfast," says he, panting. "They've taken the canoe with the gasoline kicker!"

"What for? "I says, which Concha does not care a thing about canoeing. It is not fun to her. She did enough of it in the old days to keep her pacified the rest of her life.

"Has Concha been talking about Centeotl?" says he, distracted.

"No," I says, which they do not talk much about their gods. "Not to me. Why? What about it?"

"She has to Gene," says Jimmy. "Been at her to go and pray so the baby will be born strong and brave. Gene told me so. But she laughed, Uncle Lew! She seemed to think it was just one of Concha's quaint ideas!"

"They are not quaint," I says, "to Concha. But surely you don't think she got Gene to take stock in it?"

"No," says Jimmy, groaning. "I—I don't know. You know how queer she's been!"

He did not notice the men standing there: I did not realize, myself, till afterward; but three of them could talk English—a German shift boss named Miller, and a half-white Mexican from Ixtlan, and a white hobo named Charley Something. Last year we had a regular plague of hobos drifting down from the railroad camps north of Tepic, and they was pretty sick of hoboing by the time they hit our camp; but they seldom stayed long enough to learn their last names. Not that it matters what his name was now!

Afterward I remembered them standing there with both ears stuck up like jack rabbits. Plenty of people have heard yarns about Guatamo's gold.

"It's all my fault," says Jimmy, cursing. "I don't know how I came to tell her. But I didn't want her to be worried. I didn't tell her how much gold there was. I didn't tell her I was lucky to get away alive. I told her they wouldn't have hurt me if I hadn't been shooting at a sacred crane. Of course she was curious about Guatamo's cave—who wouldn't be? It seemed to amuse her, and God knows she's had little enough—"

That was the truth. Gene is an active kid and she had been cooped up till she felt like she would yell; and she got to thinking about that wonderful cave which—

"She doesn't realize," says Jimmy, "how they live on hair trigger day and night. I just made a sort of Arabian Nights of it. I never thought—I told her how Guatamo said I could get to him if I ever wanted to see him again—by the river, but alone—one at a time, the way the Indians come. He told me what to say, and I told her that too. It seemed to tickle her. She said it over till she learned it. Said she was going to try it. But she laughed, I tell you! I thought she was just kidding! I—"

"Sure she was," I says. " Likely she has forgot all about it by now."

"No," says Jimmy. "She said she was going—today."

That is one trouble with joshing; you can say a thing and nobody will believe you. Gene, she did not want him to believe her; she knew it was not sensible; but she got to thinking about it, like Gonzalo's wife and the ice cream, and it sounded easy—just step down to the river and into the canoe. More like a picnic. She claims it seemed right reasonable at the time.

I am not blaming Concha. She fairly worships Gene, but she is an Indian and she thought it was the thing to do.

Whew! Gentlemen, that is not my idea of a picnic. I tried to get the kid to leave his gun at home, which if it came to fighting we could kill some of them all right, but it would not do us any good if the rest of them killed Gene and Concha. But he was fairly crazy; you could not tell him anything. He was saddled and gone before I even caught my horse. I lit out after him, and once I saw him about a mile up the trail, and thought I saw a naked Indian running by him.

I never once thought to look behind me. That is rough—Huh?

Oh, certainly, sir. Go right ahead.

Telephones are quite a thing, huh? I reckon you and your friend are used to them, but they still give me quite a feeling. They have a telephone from Siete Minas clear to Orendain, near fifty miles as the crow flies, and they tell me you can hear a man cough. So I reckon it is nothing much to talk right here in the same city. Do you reckon his friend can hear him now, low as he is talking?

Not So, Bolivia

VI

OH, THAT is all right, sir. I have got nothing but time. Where did I leave off? Oh, yes, about this naked Indian running by Jimmy's stirrup. Those fellows can sure run; and they can keep it up all day, fast as a horse can go on trails like those. That is rough going; a horse cannot get through some of those *barrancas*; you have to climb out and go around by the mesa and in again. It kept me busy trying to catch up without breaking my horse's neck.

And I did not catch up. Not so, Bolivia! That boy was going two jumps to my one; he did not give a durn for any horse's neck; not then. I was four miles behind when he shot over the edge and went rocketing down that canyon wall, and if that Indian was still with him, I bet he was saying "Now I lay me[122]" to Huitzil'. But I

---

122 Now I lay me. A classic children's bedtime prayer from the 18th century. Full verse as follows:

> *Now I lay me down to sleep,*
> *I pray the Lord my Soul to keep;*
> *If I should die before I 'wake,*
> *I pray the Lord my Soul to take.*

Uncle Lew used this well-known verse to indicate the Indian's concern for his life.

White Fox Wades Out About Twenty Feet and Shows Me Where to Turn

did not find them dead at the bottom. Time I got down to where his horse was killed that other time, I could not see a soul.

I knew the cave was somewhere in that neighborhood. And he had come this way; I could see places where a horse's calks[123] had scratched the rock. But it is just a shelf above the river, and it rears up at one end, sharp as a church roof; no horse could climb it. And there was rocks and bushes that would hide a man, but not a horse. I kept expecting arrows any minute. I did not know what to do. Up on the far hills you could still see the sun, but in that deep crack it was already dusk. Blue dusk, and water gurgling under tall cliffs like it has gurgled for ten thousand years, and blue sky empty as a dead man's eyes.

All of a sudden I heard a woman screaming. Faint and far off, but clear as glass until those echoes took it up and turned it into ghostly laughing; and I am telling you my hair stood up. I have heard mountain cats yell for forty years, and it sounds something like a woman being hurt bad; but I never heard a cat scream, "Jimmy! I can't stand it!"

I knew too much about the way they worship to their gods; or used to, when they had the prisoners. Huitzil' especially; he is their war god, and a cruel bloody one. But I could not find a hole a mouse could get into, much less a horse.

And there was an Indian standing at my elbow. That is, he was naked like one, and brown as one, only this cloth around his middle and a band of gold around his head. But his muscles bulged under his skin, which an Indian's do not unless he is overworked or old; and this White Fox is young. He is not more than twenty-one or two. And his hair is black, but kind of curly, which an Indian's is not, and his eyes are gray—blue gray, and blaze cold like a white man's when he hates you.

I thought he was going to fly at me. I did not know he was hating me just because I was Jimmy's partner—account of Naya, I mean. He is the one she is engaged to marry. He will be king when old Guatamo dies, if ever.

---

123 Calks. Or 'caulkins'. Blunt spikes on horseshoes to prevent slipping.

But he had got his orders from Guatamo. I do not know how they find out just what is happening, but they do. They knew I was trailing Jimmy, and they knew Miller and the half-breed and this Charley hobo was trailing me.

He snarls something at me in Nahua—but he can talk Spanish pretty good when he wants to, White Fox can; and he does not talk in his throat like an Indian, but in his mouth like a white man. His voice is deep but kind of sweet. And, gentlemen, you ought to hear that White Fox sing! You would not think so much voice could come out of any man. Not loud, I mean; just much; I can't explain. More like out in the woods where trees are big, and the wind singing deep and all around you. They say he makes up his own songs. They say it is a gift from one of his great-great-grand-pas that was named Coyotl too; but one of them was a white man or I miss my guess.

Huh? Yes, the cave is just beyond that ridge sticking out of the canyon wall. Yes, you can get into it horseback if you know the way, but you will drown yourself if you do not. I was just going to tell you. White Fox, he jumps into the river and motions me to slide my horse down quick. He wades out about twenty feet and shows me where to turn, and upstream and in behind this ridge, and pulls my horse behind some big rocks in the water and motions me to hold my breath.

Gentlemen, I held it. Because there was six-eight Indians perching around with arrows on their bowstrings, and one of them pulled his arrow back and pointed it at me. Those big bows are something to hold back; they will drive an arrow through a bull: but I do not know how long we waited, and nobody moved a muscle. That is why Indians are so good at hiding. They can be in plain sight and you will not see them because they do not move.

That cave is sure a bad place to slip up on. There in front of it where we was standing, the echoes bring you every rock that rolls. I thought it was a regiment of cavalry, but it was just one horse. That German and the half-breed, they was willing to let Charley take the chances while they stayed back up on the cliff and watched. Or maybe they could not hold him back. Maybe he thought he was going to bulge right in and get himself a chunk of gold and never fool with working any more.

I heard him go into the river like I did, but he missed the place and went plunk into deep water. I heard his horse climb out and gallop off; but he had lost Charley. I heard him splash and sputter for a minute, and then I could not hear a thing.

Those Indians could; I saw their eyes. And sure enough, that fool hobo come creeping up that ridge and stuck his head over right where they was watching. One of the arrows snicked the rock and went sailing up into the sky, but two of them drilled square into his skull. I remember those two bright feathers hanging down.

I bet his friends got tired waiting for him to move.

So White Fox took me on into the cave. The others did not go; you know, it is a sacred place … Huh? Yes, it is right there behind these rocks. Yes, you could go by in a canoe and never see it. The mouth is nearly under water—Lord knows how deep on one side. It is a lake underground; a big spring, I reckon, because the water is ice cold, though you do not notice any current because it is so deep. I remember how I shivered—pitch dark and windy, and me wet to the waist and not too easy in my mind. I felt the roof go up, and saw lights high in the air, and heard the slow, thin voice of old Guatamo crying to Huitzil'.

Huh? Yes, it is high inside. There is quite a *teocalli*[124] by the shore of the lake—a temple of their gods; a pyramid with steps on all four sides, the sacrificial stone on top, and idols and altars with the everlasting fire. It must be near a hundred feet up to these cracks in the cliff where the morning sun strikes through and shines on this big statue of Huitzil', and the roof is somewhere above that. It is a place where strata rock has buckled and heaved up—two hundred feet, to judge from the outside.

Yes, you can see the buckle in the face of the cliff. It runs all the way up to the mesa rim. That ridge sticking out is part of it, and these big rocks in the water are pieces that broke off.

---

124 Teocalli. God-house; a temple on top a pyramid.

Sir? Yes, that canyon has a name. No, sir, I did not say.

Oh, sure; no harm in wondering. Many a man has.

I am right glad I met up with you gentlemen. Jimmy, he has got friends here, but they are young fellows and seem to think I have got one foot in the grave. I do not know what to say to them. They are so busy just—just being young; I can't explain. Working and joshing and thinking what they are going to do tomorrow. They never seem to wonder what these hills could tell.

You catch a glimpse of it sometimes. Men rising up through centuries to lead them on, and leaving names that men remember yet—like giants moving somewhere in the mist.

Take their god Quetzal'[125]—there is a statue of him in that cave. He was not cruel like their fighting god Huitzil'. He had blue eyes and yellow hair. And whiskers; yellow ones, or so the story goes. The Fair God, they called him. Now where did they get that idea, a thousand years before they ever saw a white man? He came from the Eastern Sea[126], where Vera Cruz is now, and taught them to plant corn and take care of the sick ones and live decent. He had a long staff with a winged snake in silver on it; that is what Quetzalcoatl means, Feathered Snake; but I have heard it was the sign of a doctor in Europe or somewhere once. He tried to get them to stop human sacrifice, and Huitzil' picked a quarrel with him and he had to leave the country. He went back into the sunrise on a raft made out of snakes—live ones; or so the story goes.

But you know what that means. This one lone white man—he got old and maybe sick, and could not hold his own against the priests. He knew they would cut his heart out alive; he had to use some trick to get away—some magic to keep them thinking he was a god. He told them he was coming back, and after he was gone they realized how good he was, and kept expecting him six hundred years.

---

125 Quetzal'. Quetzalcoatl, Aztec feather-serpent god of life, light, wisdom, and the winds, and more; a major deity.

126 Eastern Sea. Gulf of Mexico.

You cannot keep from wondering who he was. You cannot keep from wondering where he died, out on his raft alone, when he had done the best he could for them.

Columbus was a tenderfoot compared to him. He makes a heap of difference today. Because the Spaniards came, and one of them had blue eyes and yellow whiskers, and the people said Quetzal' had come and brought his friends along, and the priests claimed it was no use to fight against the gods. Maybe the Spaniards could have licked them anyway; but I do not believe it. I hear they had a hard time as it was.

Sir? No, this statue of Quetzal' is not pure gold; it is gold on copper; it tings like a bell when you tap it. It is squat and ugly, like they thought gods ought to look, but I admit I said a little prayer to him—for him, I mean. I know he was not a god, but he was a brave man and nobody will ever know.

Yes, the statue of Huitzil' is solid. Yes, it is better than life size; the tip of his war bonnet stands near seven feet, and he is thicker than a man. But if you are in a hurry, gentlemen—

No, sir, I do not want a drink.

Yes, Gene was in there. Getting off my horse, I stumbled and fell over something, and it was her canoe pulled up on the shore. I nicked my shin against the gasoline kicker, and I can't tell you what a feeling it gave me—this bright chunky little piece of machinery in that spooky place where everything was cruel and dark and old.

Blind as a bat, I was. Going by that pyramid, I pretty near stepped off into that black ice-cold lake. White Fox, he caught me; quick as a cat, he is; and strong? He pretty near unjointed my backbone. He lugged me up a rocky slope, and there was doors cut in the wall and a light showing through feather curtains. I stepped too high and stumbled in and pretty near knocked Jimmy over.

It would not have took much. The boy was white around the gills and pretty shaky, but he tried to grin.

"You—you're just in time," says he. It's a—"

Huh? Sure, I will be glad to meet any friend of yours. Howdy do, doctor? I am pleased to meet you, sir. Have a chair. Huh? Well, maybe a little drink would not do us any harm; but you cannot buy it. Not so, Bolivia! This is on me. I was just telling them, doctor, about the time my partner's son was born.

It was quite a surprise, which we was not expecting the little rascal for a—Sir?

Yes, that is right. Yes, I have seen the cave myself. No, sir, I do not mind describing it; if you can find it and get out alive, you will know as much as I do. Here is the tunnel going in. Here is where it narrows and they can drop rocks on you. Here is this black lake—I do not know how big; it is too dark to see. Here is this temple on the shore … Huh? No, just a pyramid with all their gods on top. Here the ground runs up to doors cut into the back part where they live. Bedrooms you might call them; I was just telling these gentlemen—that is where my partner woke up one time when he got an arrow through his shoulder and fell over the cliff.

Well, you can imagine, doctor. He expected to wake up dead, but there he was on a soft mat with a feather canopy over him, and gold and silver everywhere, and a beautiful girl down on her knees, fanning and staring at him with her big, solemn black eyes.

"Hello!" says Jimmy. "Where are we, and if so, who?"

VII

BUT Nayanenetzin—her name is Naya, doctor; *tzin* means she is royalty, and *nene* means baby or child, because she is not married yet—she does not talk English or Spanish either; and Jimmy does not talk Nahua, but he did not give a durn. You know how young fellows are with pretty girls. He talked to her anyway, joshing and laughing because she did not understand.

Naya, she did not know what to make of him at first. They do not do much laughing around there. It is a sad place when you come to think of it. It is not only a church; it is all that is left of an empire and the glory of long centuries gone by.

But you do not know my partner, doctor. First thing you know, he had her smiling too. It must have been a novelty to her—born and raised in that dark and gloomy place; I reckon she never saw the open sunshine in her life; her skin is barely coppered, though she is pure Indian. She is right beautiful. She has got big eyes and a soft baby mouth that looks like she has never laughed; but Jimmy, he trained her. That is their name for him—Laughing White Man.

He would laugh and call her sweetheart, and she would just come running, all fixed to smile for him.

She is a tall girl, and you do not realize how young she is until she smiles—more like a baby, though she is thirteen and going to be married. She did not know what "sweetheart" meant, but White Fox did; he can talk Spanish pretty good: and he felt like carving—Huh? No, I am just calling him White Fox because these gentlemen seem to think there is something tricky about saying Ixtaccicoyotl, which is his name. He is the prince and Naya is engaged to him.

You cannot blame him for hating Jimmy. I noticed his eyes, but I did not know what he was sore about till one day I heard a sort of commotion, and there was him and Jimmy all tangled up and rolling on the ground like a pair of—Huh?

Oh, four-five days. If you are a doctor you will know that Gene could not travel right away; but she is a healthy girl and—Huh? Well, maybe it was longer. I did not keep track exactly.

Yes, they let us stay. Yes, I got to know it pretty good. Sir? Oh, ten or twelve, I reckon; their war god and their harvest god and their sun god and their wind god and—I forget. Huitzil', he seems to be the main one. He is their fighting god. They say he was born with his hands full of arrows and humming-bird feathers on his left leg—that is what Huitzilopochtli means, Feathers on the Left—and jumped right up and chased his grown brothers into the lake and drowned them. Yes, for a baby, he must have been quite a fighter.

Sir? Well, he is kind of thick and ugly. No, sir, I do not remember exactly. Just ugly, like all their idols … No, sir, I could not say … Yes, it seems to me there was … No, I cannot be sure … Well, here is these altars on the pyramid and the gods kind of standing around. No, I do not remember just how. Yes, there is quite a lot of writing. The walls of the main cave are covered with it as high as a man can reach … No, sir, I do not remember … Guatamo, he would read it by the hour, and White Fox would say it in Spanish for us, but I could not make head or tail of it. Kings doing this and that, the year so-and-so of Fish or Rabbit, and signs curled up if the king said yes, and down if he said no. And—Oh, yes; signs like on this gold piece. This gentleman seemed to think it was a piece of money, but—

Yes, that is what I told him … You know about the Nahuas, doctor?

Well, I will be durned! What is the use of me telling you when you know more about it than I do? I thought Guatamo was the only man alive that could still read their writing. I am proud to know you, sir! *Deveras es un gusto dar con uno á quién no la extraña lo que*[127] —Oh, I thought you talked Spanish. How come you can read Aztec writing then?

I did not mean to hurt your feelings, doctor; I was just saying it is a pleasure to meet a man that knows. Yes, sure there is a difference between studying a thing and just hearing yarns. All I know is what my wife has told me, one time or another in the last thirty years. No, she is not an Aztec; she is a Chichimec, which is an older—Sir?

No, sir. She did not tell me about the cave; I just finished telling you I was there … No, sir, I cannot be sure … No, I did not notice exactly. All I know is just what I am telling you.

Well, sir, that is your business. I cannot help whether you believe it or not.

Yes, far as I know, we are the only white men that ever did.

Sir? Oh, yes; I forgot to tell you. Miller and the half-breed, they must have realized finally that something had happened to Charley. So they got away from there. They got a few roughnecks to help them—white men; you could not hire an Indian—and waited for a dark night and slipped into the tunnel. They did not know it was fixed for that. I heard a smashing and yelling and—Sir?

Well, not all at once. Finally, yes.

H-s-st! Waiter! See what the gentlemen will have.

No, sir, they did not get the gold. Not so, Bolivia! They made a game try, but that cave is a bad place to tackle. First off, you cannot get into that canyon without some Indian knowing it. If it is too dark for arrows, they just wait till you get into the tunnel, and just touch a button and down comes fifty tons of rock.

---

127 Deveras es un gusto dar con uno á quién no la extraña lo que—. "It really is a pleasure to find one who is not surprised by what—"

Drink hearty, gentlemen!

No, it did not kill them all. It smashed the first boat all right, but Miller and three-four of them swum out and started shooting, and the second boat slipped in because they cannot drop the rock but once. Seem-like the cave was full of them, shooting and yelling. I grabbed my pants and gun and galloped out and—See this scar? That is where an arrow gashed me, whining by. Indians was fairly pouring in from the back part of the cave. No, they do not live in there; not all of them; only Guatamo and his priests and kinfolks, like Naya and her mother and White Fox. But there is a tunnel winding up two thousand feet and out on the mesa, and the alarm got to this pueblo I was telling you about.

The robbers had got up on the pyramid and was shooting from behind the gods. You could see fire spitting out, but nothing to shoot at, till all of a sudden a light blazed out from everywhere. No, not electric light; you could not see where it came from … No, sir, I do not know if they touch a button or what … Yes I know they touch a button for the rock; I looked it over afterward.

Yes, they have any number of tricks; I was going to tell you. But I am getting thirsty again. Where is that durn waiter?

Well, sir, that was sure a sight. This magic light that did not make a shadow; this black lake shimmering and this black pyramid looming up, gold shining on the steps where old Guatamo put his feet when they carried him up to worship; gold on the altars and jewels twinkling like in the sun, and smoke from guns mixed up with smoke from sacred fires, and the big gold idols standing there. Tons and tons of gold, and robbers using it for a shield!

The Indians did not like to shoot at their own gods. White Fox, he started up the steps with nothing but a knife, and Miller leaned out to take a shot at him; but Jimmy drilled him. Miller come tumbling down and White Fox grabbed him up, though Miller was a big man, and held him over his shoulders to stop the bullets, and come galloping back to thank Jimmy for saving his life. They was good friends after that; but Miller was shot full of holes.

That was when I saw the water rising. White Fox had to splash through it, coming back. Up and up, covering the pyramid a step at a time. Up and up the slope toward the doors at the back of the cave; but it did not quite reach us. They have got it figured to a gnat's heel. That pyramid was under water while the bedrooms was still dry.

Yes, sure it drowned the sacred fires: but they put them out every fifty-two years anyway, and they did not dare to let those fellows out alive … Huh? No, the arrows put some of them out of their misery, but some of them swum out of range and—

Huh?

Say, young fellow, I bet your mamma did not teach you to come butting in where gentlemen are talking. I reckon you are one of the young dudes Jimmy introduced me to, but I do not give a durn. If you want to see me, you can sit over there and wait till we are through, or you can take a walk and cool yourself off. Just suit yourself.

Excuse me, gentlemen. Young fellows have not got any manners nowadays. Where did I leave off? Oh, yes, these fellows being drowned. Some of them tried to swim out, but the tunnel was thirty feet under water by that time. We could see them struggling quite a while; but finally they all went under, and the water went down and the Indians gathered up their bodies, because that lake is where they get their drinking water.

No, I do not know why they do not keep that light on all the time. I would if it was me.

Whose turn is it to buy a drink?

No, nothing much happened after that. Yes, they showed us a real good time. They give us a banquet every day, old Guatamo sitting on his throne, and a beautiful girl to wait on Jimmy and another one on me. Oh, yes, and when Gene was able to travel, they give us a pocketful of gold trinkets. See this thunder-bird charm? That is one of them …

No, sir, I never have been back. I always meant to, but I never seemed to get around to it.

Well, if nobody else will buy a drink, I will. H-s-st! Waiter! See what the—

VIII

I WAS afraid you could not keep your face straight, Jimmy. This doctor, he asked a million questions about that cave, and I thought he was just interested; but finally he started getting funny. I was telling him about Miller and the half-breed trying to slip into the tunnel, and the watchman on that shelf dropping rocks and knocking the bottom out of their boat; but Mister Doctor cut his eyes sideways at his friends and smiled sarcastic and polite.

"And the robbers were all killed!" says he.

Kind of mocking me, you know. He thought I was making it up; so I made him up a good one while I was at it. I had them touching buttons and dropping rock fifty tons at a time. I had the water coming and drowning them off the pyramid—fifteen or forty of them; I forget. He would not think it was anything just to have your boat sunk and be shot full of arrows.

He would not think it was anything to make friends with Ixtac-cicoyotl by wrestling with him and grinning like a man when he could throw you every time. Not so, Bolivia! If anybody asks you, Ixtaccicoyotl is a friend of yours because you saved his life.

No, much obliged, Jimmy. I have had more drinks already than I wanted; but that is not what makes me feel like laughing.

I was just thinking of stylish banquets in that cave, and beautiful girls waiting on us. Yes, sir!

You could not tell those fellows in a million years. Naya, for instance; they would see that she was a beautiful child, but they would not see the pity of it—even if she smiled for them, timid and wishful like she does. Or Ixtaccicoyotl; they would see he is a handsome fellow and a slick wrestler; but they would not wonder where he got that big deep voice of his, or the blood that makes him look and act like a white man when he is supposed to be pure Aztec royalty.

But they would be hot dog after that gold.

Huh? Well, let them hunt. I told them it was on a river, and there is not more than six of them in twenty miles of our place. I told them it was under a buckle in the cliff, and if they can find a hundred yards of cliff that is not buckled I will eat your hat. And if they stumble onto it—well, they can never say I did not tell them. They will leave their skulls with Miller and that Charley hobo, and without any fancy touches either. Which they have got a perfect right to do.

But do not worry, Jimmy. They think I am a windy old liar from the word go. I saw their faces, and it was worth the price. They do not believe a man could know about that gold and keep his hands off. They do not know you, Jimmy. They do not know Gene, and they have never seen that son of yours. They do not know what well off is. They would know all about a million dollars, but Indians are just peons to them; and they would not see that being square has made you and your wife and son a million friends.

Ho-hum! Well, come on, Jimmy. It must be nearly ten o'clock. Cities may be all right for them that likes excitement, but not me. Not so, Bolivia! I will sure be glad when morning comes and we are started home.

APPENDIX

From the Editor's Desk

In the course of my extensive research, I unearthed a fantastic amount of information about C. E. Scoggins, his illustrator, his work, and his times, including some fascinating facts about the history of the mining district of the Mexican State of Jalisco.

I've included the best of my research for your enjoyment. We begin with a brief biography of Scoggins that I compiled from numerous sources. One of the best things about him was that he was the Real Deal—he was born in Mexico and spent much of his life working in Latin America.

His illustrator, W. H. D. Koerner, was prolific and popular in his time. One of his paintings hung in the U. S. White House during the Bush presidency.

I've included another short biography written by Scoggins himself, which will give you a glimpse of his charm, wit, and humor.

We conclude with three short segments about Mexico in the 1920s, just after the Mexican Revolution. Many Americans, Canadians, and Europeans were heavily invested in the Mexican economy—fortunes were made and lost by the score.

I hope that you enjoy the background information as much as I have, and especially that it should enhance your enjoyment of these two stories.

Charles Elbert Scoggins
Biography

Born in Mazatlán, Sinaloa, Republic of Mexico in 1888 to American Methodist-missionary parents, young Charles Elbert Scoggins grew up in what has been called the Age of Storytellers. This was the age of H. Rider Haggard, Robert Louis Stevenson, Sir Arthur Conan Doyle, Rudyard Kipling, H.G. Wells, and many more. Today, we can only imagine what it must have meant to young Elbert to get his hands on English-language literature of his day.

There seems little doubt that he was familiar with the works of those storytellers, as he described himself as a "passionate reader." Many of his stories are of the "Lost World" genre, which includes H. Rider Haggard's *King Solomon's Mines* (1885), Rudyard Kipling's *The Man Who Would Be King* (1888), Arthur Conan Doyle's *The Lost World* (1912), Edgar Rice Burroughs' *The Land That Time Forgot* (1918).

The "Lost World" genre arose during an era when the fascinating remnants of lost civilizations around the world were being discovered, such as the tombs of Egypt's Valley of the Kings, the semi-mythical stronghold of Troy, the jungle-shrouded pyramids of the Maya, and the cities and palaces of the empire of Assyria. Thus, real stories of archaeological finds by imperial adventurers succeeded in capturing the public's imagination.

Scoggins' lost-civilization stories and many more tales are about Americans in Central and South America. One editor has noted that a good case could be made that one of his characters, Colin O'Leary, was the prototype, or at least a prototype, of Indiana Jones, fedora and all.

Personal details are few: he smoked a pipe, played golf, drank alcohol, and was a Protestant. A contemporary said of him, "No picture could do Brother Scoggins justice, however. No man can meet him and fail to be impressed with his keenness of observation, his aptness of expression, and that intangible trait of character that is ordinarily called the impress of latent power and innate strength. He's tall and angular, unless he's added a lot of weight lately, and talks, as he writes, like a volley of machine gun bullets. Read his stories, and you'll get the same impression." — *The Phi Gamma Delta* magazine, February, 1923

Scoggins graduated from high school in Denton, Texas, then in 1906 became a freshman at the University of Texas, where he became a 'Fiji,' i.e., a member of the Phi Delta Gamma fraternity, a relationship that would last a lifetime. In 1907 he left the University due to 'personal considerations,' which he later described as a practical need for food and clothing. A fellow student described him as "a famous freshman, who, by his splendid cartoons in the freshman issue of the university weekly, the Texan, so aroused the ire of the freshman class' traditional enemies, that he was, after repeated attempts, captured by them, and treated to an external dose of feathers and molasses." — *The Phi Gamma Delta* magazine, April, 1906.

He married Lois Lovett Durham on December 23, 1913, in Muncie, Indiana, her home town. For a while, at least until 1920, they lived with her parents at her family home in Muncie. Later, the Scoggins family lived in Jacksonville, Florida. In 1929 they returned from a two-year sojourn in Spain, where they stayed for a while at Castillo de Santa Clara, Torremolinos, Málaga, a popular destination for artists such as Salvador Dali and other notables of the era. In 1931, Scoggins designed and commissioned a lovely Tudor-style home in Boulder, Colorado, called Sea Horse Hill.

Their daughter, Nancy Josephine, was born in 1915. Scoggins mentioned that she was eight years old in a 1923 interview. — *The Phi Gamma Delta* magazine, February, 1923. Nancy graduated from Stanford University, School of Letters, English, in 1936.

Nancy studied Spanish at the University of Colorado, Boulder, in 1932, together with her mother. Very little more is known about Nancy, though she did have one short story, "The Nun Who Met the Rebels," in the *Liberty Magazine* issue of October 24, 1936.

Scoggins was active in a number of social organizations, such as the Authors League of America (now the Authors Guild), the Rotary Club, Cactus Club, Denver Country Club, Town and Gown, and of course his beloved fraternity, Phi Gamma Delta (Fijis).

He was a member of the staff of the Writer's Conference at the University of Colorado at Boulder from 1933 to 1955. In later life, he served as a Director of the First National Bank of Boulder. — *Who's Who in America*, 1950-1951

Lois, too, was active in community affairs, including Red Cross and the Boulder County Hospital Board. She was involved with Planned Parenthood and the local Episcopal Church.

Charles Elbert Scoggins passed away in Boulder, Colorado on December 5, 1955 at age 67. After the death of her husband, Lois became the housemother of the Delta Tau Delta Fraternity of the University of Colorado at Boulder. Lois passed away in Boulder on March 19, 1968 at the age of 78.

W. H. D. Koerner Biography

Wilhelm Heinrich Detlev "Big Bill" Koerner was born in what is now Germany in November of 1878. His family relocated to Clinton, Iowa, when he was three years old. At age 20, he became a staff artist for the Chicago Tribune.

He worked for several other periodicals while continuing his art studies at the Art Students League in New York. Koerner specialized in Western themes, and eventually produced over 500 paintings and illustrated over 200 stories and serials.

He was a frequent contributor to *The Saturday Evening Post*. He traveled extensively throughout the American West, often on horseback, sketching and studying his subject matter.

Much to his credit, Koerner was known as an artist who respected both the authors for whom he illustrated and their stories. He studied the stories and their characters in order to determine what the author intended, and his illustrations enhanced each story without distracting from it or giving away the ending. This is no small feat.

One of his paintings, *A Charge to Keep*, became the cover of George W. Bush's autobiography by the same name. The original painting was hung in the Oval Office during the Bush Presidency.

We have included the original three illustrations for *The Proud Old Name* as it appeared in the *Saturday Evening Post*. The frontispiece, "—But I Might Have Known," also appeared as the frontispiece of the 1925 book edition. These illustrations are now in the public domain.

Scoggins Tells His Own Story

Fiji Author Calls Brothers "Zulus"
(Reprinted from
The Phi Gamma Delta Magazine,
February 1923)

Unmistakable Fraternity Reference in Story in *Red Book*
by Charles Elbert Scoggins of Texas Chapter
By Hargrave A. Long (Chicago '11)

WIVES are responsible for a lot of things, good and bad, in this vale of tears and cheers, and among those many things is this article. In the first place, my wife reads the Red Book, and when she climbed through the November, 1922, issue she insisted that I read a certain story entitled: "'Keg' Henderson Learns a Song."

It dealt with the unfortunate experiences of a tramp engineer in one of the Central American countries, and the hero, "Keg" Henderson, came to a happy end because the villain in the piece turned out to be a brother "Zulu" from Tau chapter and wore a fraternity pin which the author sentimentally described as "delicately wrought of black enamel and gold, bearing three Greek letters on its face." In fact, the "Zulu" pins of two men played an important part in the plot.

And the author is a Fiji—Charles Elbert Scoggins (Texas '09), now a resident of Muncie, Indiana. He insists that he acquired the writing "bug" long before he lived in the Hoosier state. Old friends, however, attribute his increasing literary success to the Indiana atmosphere and to his long years of association with Hoosiers, especially his wife, Lois Lovett Durham Scoggins, a native of Muncie. Indiana. (And, by the way, let me add with pride, an old sweetheart of mine. Now will you be good, Elbert!)

A lot of funny happenings might be told about Brother Scoggins—how he happened to meet his wife, for instance; and how he happened to win her away from the man who, way back in high school, won her away from me; and all that sort of thing; but Elbert is a writer and makes money by it, so why not let him tell his own story, even though he didn't mean to? In this way, the readers of The Phi Gamma Delta will obtain about $2,500 worth of real literature, all for the price of one subscription. That's why I wrote Elbert for certain important biographical information about himself, and got the following:

Elbert Tells His Story

"You can't fuss me with all that bull! I was born shy and am still as bashful as the violet, but my education (see tertiary below) has taught me the advisability of taking and absorbing without hesitation all the flattering remarks I find lying around loose. At least they feel good while I'm swallowing them. I blush; of course, I blush, but nobody has ever caught me doing it.

"Born? Yes, on the 17th of Ireland, at Mazatlan, state of Sinaloa, Republic of Mexico, 1888, to Jefferson Davis Scoggins and Katherine Grant Scoggins. Father was a Methodist missionary. (Editorial Note: This explains a lot of things.) It may be gathered from his name that he was born South of the Mason and Dixon Line; so was mother, nee Grant. My maternal grandfather was related to U. S., but was deeply ashamed of the relationship, not only because U. S. was a Yankee, but also because he drank red licker or anything else he could get. (I have much of the Grant in me.)

C.E. Scoggins

(Texas '09)

All Sorts of Education

"Where have I lived? Mazatlan, Guadalajara, and a few other places in Mexico; Guthrie, Oklahoma; Bonita, Henrietta, Austin, Ballinger, and Denton, Texas; some place in New Mexico I was too young to remember; Jacksonville, Florida, and Muncie, Indiana. I may be overlooking a few, but these I can swear to. The rest of my time I was just running around.

"Education? Primary: Any school I could get into, graduating at Denton High School and continuing at the University of Texas, where I became a Fiji. Secondary: Railroad construction camps in Mexico. Tertiary: Selling Simonds saws in Cuba, Georgia, Florida, Mexico, and Central America. Finishing : Getting married and settling down to write for a living. This last stage of my education is still going on.

"So far as preparing for writing is concerned, about all I can say is that as a kid I read everything I could get away from its owner—and still do so—and secondarily, one gets a lot by just being alive and noticing that the world is full of a number of things.

"I was a Fiji at Texas, and my answer to your question as to how long I was connected with Tau Deuteron chapter is: Not half long enough. I was working my way through college, and I guess I didn't work fast enough or hard enough, or something, because

I fell out half way through, for reasons not unconnected with a habit I formed early in life of wearing clothes and eating food more or less regularly.

"You ask me for the names of some of my stories. I can't remember them all. Some of the recent ones in the Saturday Evening Post included 'Charles Frederic Goes Easy,' 'A Song in the Night,' 'The Man Who Never Smiled,' and some others that may be in print before this. The Red Book is running a series of railroad construction stories, beginning in the November issue, the one you read, I guess.

"My hobby? Writing stories. Ambition? To write good ones. Vices? Well, I smoke a pipe; I play what looks like, from a distance, golf; and—huh? Well, I don't mind if I do; but a fellow has to be careful these days; where did you get it?

"I mustn't forget to admit that I'm married. I leave it to you to mention her name, but I do want to insist that she was born into a Beta family and used to think she was a Beta girl, but I was always one to leap to the aid of a damsel in distress; that's me all over. She recovered, and now the only whistle she answers to is the Fiji. One daughter, Nancy Josephine, eight years old—and she's a houseful!

"I dare you to get my picture.

"And that's that!"

Writer-like, Elbert didn't sign his name, but he took the precaution to use his regular letterhead, with 214 North Vine St., Muncie, Indiana, 'n' everything on it. I'm pretty sure Lois—the important half of the Scoggins family—didn't write the letter, else she wouldn't have stood for the Beta reference; but if there is a picture with this article, it will be because Lois took up the "dare" and provided it.

Writes Man Stories

No picture could do Brother Scoggins justice, however. No man can meet him and fail to be impressed with his keenness of observation, his aptness of expression, and that intangible trait of character that is ordinarily called the impress of latent power and innate strength. He's tall and angular, unless he's added a lot of weight lately, and talks, as he writes, like a volley of machine gun bullets. Read his stories, and you'll get the same impression.

All in all, Elbert is a man's man, and his stories are always about real "he"-men—sailors sometimes, or saw-mill men, or railroad construction men, or down and outers who won't stay down and out, and so forth. I fancy Elbert has been, one time or another, each of the men he describes in his stories. I could let my language roam carelessly and compare him with Jack London in the vividness of their expressions of life in the raw, and not be very far wrong. And yet, every once in a while, there gleams a tender whimsicality or bit of sentiment in Elbert's yarns that show a sparkle of diamond in the strength of steel.

Elbert has always thought a lot of his Fiji membership. His travels have usually kept him away from the centers of Fiji numbers, but I venture the opinion that he has met more Fijis in the out of the way parts of the world than any brother of his years. While he lived in Jacksonville, Florida, just getting his feet on the lower rungs of the ladder of literature, he organized a graduate chapter there and vitalized it into a most lively and effective alumni group, with the initiative to land Charlie Eastman, alumni secretary, from Chicago, as a speaker. In Muncie he is one of the several active Fiji workers who have unitedly made Muncie "safe for Phi Gamma Delta."

Watch for the name of "C. E. Scoggins" and be sure you will find the story readable, interesting, unconventional, and gripping—all the more so because the author is a brother Fiji, and proud of it!

Romance in Old Mexico — A Review of The Proud Old Name

(Reprinted from
The Phi Gamma Delta Magazine,
December 1925)

The Phi Gamma Delta Bookshelf
Romance in Old Mexico
By William J. Aiken (Allegheny '09)

In his chummy little romance, The Proud Old Name, C. E. Scoggins (Texas '08) has written one of the best books of the year. Without a useless phrase the plot moves swiftly through entertaining situations to a surprising close. Old Mexico and a proud old don, the Don Santiago Moreno, lord of a vast estate, his daughter, a soft-eyed senorita ineffably lovely, a dashing, adventuresome Yankee named Jimmy Brown, who, besides falling in love with adorable daughters of Venus, employed his time as a mining engineer—these afford the characters to start the plot. Santiago Moreno, proud of his ancient name and lineage, learns that this name translated into English is Jimmy Brown and looks with favor upon his daughter's marriage to the young American. Then upon the scene appears one day in a storm a flapper from the States, accompanied by her father. The plot thickens immediately. Jimmy Brown's plans to marry the Senorita Morena meet an unexpected change. The end is as exciting as the finish of a hard-run quarter-mile.

In telling the tale briefly Brother Scoggins is conforming to what seems to be the present day idea of correct form for novels. A few years ago an English or an American writer would have extended the same plot through a volume of six or seven hundred pages, and then added a sequel. Not until the reaction against modern speed and restlessness sets in will people have the leisure to read a novel of the old school. Action and condensation, — Les Miserables, Don Quixote, Vanity Fair, A Tale of Two Cities, abridged into a movie film of an hour and a half or less, such is the demand of the moment. The Proud Old Name meets the present demand and is a commendable bit of literature. Homely humor, lively narrative, abundant action, and real plot, a very large book done up in a small package.

Other Works by Charles Elbert Scoggins

Novels

The Proud Old Name, 1924

The Red Gods Call, 1926, aka The Country of Old Men

White Fox, 1928

John Quixote, 1929

The Walking Stick, 1930

The House of Darkness, 1931

Flame, 1931

Tycoon, 1932

The House of Dawn, 1934 ("Colin O'Leary" Series)

Pampa Joe, 1935

Lost Road, 1941 ("Colin O'Leary" Series)

The Strangers, 1945

Other Works

The Voice of Things Forgotten (short story),
The Green Book Magazine Feb 1918

The Breath of Onions (short story),
Smith's Magazine Aug 1918

Place to Sleep (short story),
Collier's Dec 7 1918

Jerry Remembers Something (short story),
The Saturday Evening Post Jan 25 1919

And So to Bed (short story),
Collier's Jun 7 1919

Thanks to the Dog (short story),
Collier's Jun 21 1919

Henry Becomes a Pet (short story),
Romance May 1920

The Ingenious Senor 'Oogis (short story),
The Red Book Magazine Jan 1922

The Whiskers of the King (short story),
People's Story Magazine Apr 10 1922

Charles Frederic Goes Easy (short story),
The Saturday Evening Post Apr 22 1922

A Song in the Night (short story),
The Saturday Evening Post May 20 1922

The Man Who Never Smiled (short story),
The Saturday Evening Post Sep 30 1922

Keg Henderson Learns a Song (short story),
The Red Book Magazine Nov 1922

The Gate of Mighty Dreams (short story),
The Saturday Evening Post Dec 2 1922

Three Links and a Dinger (short story),
The Red Book Magazine Dec 1922

The Hog (short story),
The Saturday Evening Post Jan 20 1923

Loose Foot (short story),
The Saturday Evening Post Feb 17 1923

Pure Reason Higgs (short story),
The Red Book Magazine Apr 1923

A Toast to the Bride (short story),
Woman's Home Companion Apr 1923

Cat's Paw (serial),
The Saturday Evening Post Aug 18 1923, etc.

Spring Fever (short story),
The Saturday Evening Post Sep 8 1923

According to His Eyes (short story),
The Saturday Evening Post Dec 29 1923

The Tumtum Tree (short story),
The Saturday Evening Post Apr 12 1924

It's Different Now (short story),
The Saturday Evening Post May 31 1924

Cherub (short story),
Woman's Home Companion May 1924

Scared Babbitt (short story),
The Red Book Magazine May 1924

Not So, Bolivia (short story),
The Saturday Evening Post Apr 24 1926

Toss—Oars! (misc),
The American Legion Monthly Oct 1926

What's Become of Sergeant York (article),
The American Legion Monthly Feb 1927

A Man Named Carrigan (short story),
The Saturday Evening Post Feb 18 1928

Jungle (short story),
The Saturday Evening Post Nov 10 1928

Man Lost (serial),
The Saturday Evening Post Oct 12 1940, etc.

The Eighth Wonder of the World [with E. T. Gilliard] (article),
The Saturday Evening Post Jul 26 1941

Hot Afternoon (short story),
The Blue Book Magazine Feb 1942

The Strangers (serial),
The Saturday Evening Post Aug 31 1946, etc.

Showdown (novelette),
The Saturday Evening Post Feb 8 1947

The Right Girl (short story),
The Saturday Evening Post Apr 17 1948

Now I Have a Son (novelette),
The Saturday Evening Post Oct 8 1949

Motion Pictures

Tycoon, 1947, Screenplay by Borden Chase, starring John Wayne, Laraine Day, Cedric Hardwicke, Judith Anderson, James Gleason, and Anthony Quinn.

Untamed, 1929. Based on the short story *Jungle*, which first appeared in The Saturday Evening Post, November 10, 1928. Starring Joan Crawford, Robert Montgomery, and Ernest Torrence.

By Nancy Scoggins

The Nun Who Met the Rebels (short story)
Liberty Oct 24 1936

Economic Development of Mexico in the Early 1900s

Beginning in 1876, with the presidency of Porfirio Díaz, Mexico welcomed investment from the United States, Canada, and Europe as a means to modernize Mexico and bring prosperity. Laws concerning subsoil rights and property rights were changed to make mining and oil production much more attractive to foreign investors.

The creation of a railway network decreased transportation costs for heavy and bulky goods. The railway network eventually served most regions of Mexico, connecting the coasts to Mexico City, and reached as far as the United States border.

In 1910, the Mexican Revolution interrupted the influx of foreign investments. Newly elected president Francisco Madero was slow to honor his somewhat vague campaign promises to return stolen village lands to the people, which prompted a revolt against the government, aimed at sweeping land reforms. American enterprises were targeted. Haciendas were seized. Railroad tracks, bridges, and trains were destroyed.

The fighting stopped in 1917, and production began again, but uncertainty and perceived risk drastically reduced foreign investments. This is the time period in which The Proud Old Name takes place. In the story, things are just getting rolling again after the revolution, but everything hasn't quite settled down yet.

As Uncle Lew put it, "That is the way with tenderfeet. They hear the revolution is over, and trains running again, and no Americans killed lately, and they expect profits to pick up and be as usual. They do not understand what the old-timers mean when they say a district is peaceable."

Land Reform in Mexico

The distribution of land in Mexico has been a divisive political issue since Cortez marched his men through Vale of Anahuac in 1521. Since the days of the Conquista, the Spanish colonization of the Americas, huge tracts of land known as land grants were handed out by the Spanish Crown and later the Mexican Government to encourage the development of the land.

Throughout Mexican history, various attempts were made to redistribute the land, sometimes in favor of the peasants. These reforms continued right up to the time The Proud Old Name takes place.

By the end of the 19th Century, large haciendas were expanding again, and many villages lost their communal lands. Many peasants who participated in the Mexican Revolution that preceded *The Proud Old Name* expected their village lands to be restored.

Mining Conditions in Mexico in the 1920s

By modern standards, working conditions in Mexican mines in the 1920s were brutal. The miners worked long days for poor wages and were often hopelessly in debt to the "company store."

There was no equivalent of OSHA to ensure safe working conditions. Heavy mining equipment was sometimes poorly maintained and hazardous. Accidents and fatalities we not uncommon.

We know this today because in 1926, a Marxist-led, Jalisco-wide union demanded better salaries and working conditions. Rather than comply, some mines simply shut down. Others shut down due to political disorder. Some were never reopened.

In *The Proud Old Name*, Uncle Lew ran an upscale operation, including smelting the ore into bullion before shipping it. He had American investors and therefore was able to run a safe, profitable operation.

About The Editor

Connor MacKenzie was born in the United States in 1956. After graduating from high school, Connor declined a medical scholarship to Stanford University. Instead, Connor traveled the world working at many jobs, including window washer, hot air balloon pilot, house painter, time-share salesman in Mexico, school bus driver, street musician, English teacher in the Dominican Republic, ranch hand, e-zine publisher, bio-diesel manufacturer, sailboat captain, carpet cleaner, pig photographer, and computer programmer. He now resides on California's North Coast, where the redwoods meet the sea.

Also by Connor MacKenzie:
The Bear and The Rose, a novel

About the Cover Artist

Daniel Wood is a freelance artist and illustrator based in Richmond, Virginia.

He honed his skills at Virginia Commonwealth University, where he earned a Bachelor of Fine Arts degree in Communication Arts. Drawing is the love of his life, so much so that he often spends his spare time drawing the day away.

Skilled in many forms of illustration, including concept art, comic art, book illustrations, and game art, both colored and black-and-white, he specializes in fantasy, science-fiction, and all of their more specific subgenres. Every project is a joyful challenge to transform the author's concepts into compelling visual imagery.

Daniel welcomes discussions regarding new projects. See more of his work at http://www.danielwoodart.com/, or e-mail him at woodillustration@gmail.com.